$50 A NIGHT

$50 A NIGHT

DON JAMES

CUTTING EDGE

ISBN-13: 978-1-970848-11-3

Published by
Cutting Edge Books
PO Box 8212
Calabasas, CA 91372
www.cuttingedgebooks.com

PROLOGUE — FRIDAY NIGHT

She had been nervous about the date from the beginning. Maybe it had been the man's voice over the telephone; a nervousness that she had detected. Or maybe it was simply a strange sense of warning that some people who live in the gray side of life seem to develop.

Because Ann Freeman was reasonably intelligent—despite her profession—she could be fairly objective about herself, her life, and her intuitions.

This was a summer Friday night in a West Coast city. She had worked every night this week, beginning with Monday night, and she should include the two afternoon dates. Ten dates in all, and this was the eleventh.

She preferred to call them "dates." It was one of the few small subterfuges she allowed herself in trying to escape reality. Most of the girls called them "tricks."

"So let's face it," she told herself. "I'm a fifty-dollar call girl, here in this hotel suite to turn a trick. And the man scares me.

She tried not to let her apprehension show and she accepted the drink the man offered her. He was a stocky man of medium height. His black hair was beginning to thin. His jaws looked heavy. He wore trousers and a soft shirt, open at the throat, with sleeves rolled up on muscular, hair-covered forearms.

It was a little after eight-thirty. They were in the sitting room of a two-room suite. The door to the bedroom was open. She had checked about the suite. They were particular in this hotel. If a man had a suite, he might be expected to have guests. They couldn't say much. Or if a man was registered with a wife, even if he was alone, there usually was little risk for a girl. The hotel people wouldn't take a chance on causing trouble. These were the ordinary things a fifty-dollar girl checked as a matter of course.

The man stood over her, drink in hand.

"I don't usually do this," he said. "Once in a while, maybe. But today I felt like it. So I called Mac and he gave me the number."

Ann sipped the drink. He had made it too strong. "I know," she smiled. "I wouldn't be here otherwise."

"Great guy, Mac. We do a lot of business together."

"You buy from him?"

"As long as he treats me right!" The man smiled more broadly. "I like the inducements. What was your name again?"

"Ann Freeman."

"You don't look like you've been in the business long."

"Not too long," Ann said lightly. How long was too long? It was three years now since the first date. Three years, and still demanding and getting fifty dollars. If you could be proud of that, then she could be proud. She watched the man's strong fingers grip his glass and she felt the apprehension again.

They both drank, Ann sparingly. She never drank much—it wasn't wise on a date. The man remained standing, looking down at her.

"You're stacked," he said. He reached out an exploratory hand. "No falsies. And I'll bet you're really a blonde."

"I'm really a blonde," she smiled. She hoped he wouldn't make a crack about being certain in a few moments. Some men seemed to be obsessed with jokes about that subject. You put up with a lot of things in "the life," but some things irritated you more than others. Really irritated you.

He didn't say anything more about the hair. Instead he stood back and critically scrutinized her face.

"You're good-looking," he said. "Short, straight nose. Blue eyes. I like your skin, too."

She was suddenly puzzled by his words. This didn't sound in character; maybe because he had such a heavy, coarse, and almost brutal look about him. Somehow it was incongruous for him to be verbally admiring her. Pawing hands would be more in keeping with his appearance.

"Drink up," he urged. "I like a girl to have a drink or two. Makes things better."

She didn't want the drink, but he was a customer. She drank the rest of the drink, and put the glass on a coffee table.

"Okay?" he asked.

She nodded and took the pills. She put them in a small handbag.

"That's an expensive-looking dress," he said. "When they're simple, they cost. It looks good on you."

He went to a table where he picked up a package and tore it open. The nervous feeling was back in the pit of Ann's stomach. This was getting to be too queer. There was something off-beat.

The man took a black brassiere and black nylon panties from the opened package and held them up.

"For you," he said.

"They're nice." Ann said. They weren't particularly nice. She prided herself upon the undergarments she wore. They were expensive and carefully selected. The garments the man—what was his name? Mr. Martin?—had selected were from a cheap store.

"Nice enough for the purpose," he said, and now he had stopped smiling. His eyes were getting the intense look that she knew so well in the eyes of men. The anticipatory look. The lust look. "I want you to go into the bedroom and undress and put them on," he said. "Call me when you're ready."

Ann got up and took the garments. "It'll only take a moment," she said.

"Good. Just put them on and stand in the middle of the room and call me. Close the door after you."

She went into the bedroom and closed the door. She stared down at the cheap garments in her hand. None of this was right. All the strange instincts she seemed to have developed over the last three years were trying to warn her. For a moment she wondered if she should leave.

"You're crazy," she told herself. "He likes girls in black undies. So give him a thrill. It's probably a ten-minute trick. Five minutes looking ... five in bed ... and that's it."

She hadn't convinced herself, but she knew that she was going through with it. It was her job and she sometimes had a feeling of pride in doing her job well. All of it was part of why she was doing what she did, and how it had all happened. At any rate, if she didn't like the way things were going, she could leave.

She had a good body. Her breasts were firm. Her thighs and hips were without surplus flesh and were smoothly rounded. She had bathed and powdered and perfumed before she had left her apartment. And now, as she slipped out of her own expensive underclothing, she smiled a little. If that was what he liked, he might have done better to see her in what she bought for herself!

She put on the transparent black brassiere and lace-trimmed panties. They were a little small for her, but he would probably like that. Finally she debated about the light and decided to leave the lamps on. The man was entitled to see what he had bought—both undergarments and woman. She stood in the center of the room.

"All right, Mr. Martin. I'm ready."

The door opened and he came in. He had removed his shirt and the slacks. He wore jockey-type shorts and nothing else. Now she saw the full muscle development of the man, the heavy mat of black hair on his body.

He stood quietly and stared at her, almost impersonally. She wondered why he wore the shorts. Possibly he liked the effect it might have in how he looked; the strong man; the muscle man. Or was it shyness? Some men were that way. She wondered and waited.

She saw his eyes follow the lines of her body. His expression was tense. There was no smile. He said nothing. She waited; feeling nothing, wanting nothing. He was paying for this and she might as well be posing for an art class.

Finally he moved, walking quickly to her.

"Stand still," he commanded. He reached forward and a hand hooked into the brassiere. He ripped it from her body and now he smiled for the first time. It was not a good smile. There was no smile in the eyes, just in the lips, and abruptly Ann felt fright again.

"You bitch," he said harshly. "I'm going to have you!"

For a moment she was confused by his words and his savageness. She had encountered men with odd desires, but there was almost an insane intensity in this man's eyes. She stood stiffly, suddenly afraid to move.

She felt his hands at her waist and then the nylon being ripped away from her body. Panic seized her and she tried to break away from him. A hand clamped over her mouth. She was lifted and thrown violently on the bed.

She glared up at him, summoning anger to overcome the fear that assailed her.

"Don't be a square," she snapped. "You're not buying anything extra because I'm not selling. You can have your money back."

He bent over her, grasping her shoulders in strong fingers, his eyes feverish in excitement.

"I know what I bought," he said softly. "I know exactly what I bought. You don't want it this way? You try to stop me!"

His head came down quickly and his teeth bit into the softness of her shoulder. She cried out in pain and struck at him in a frightened burst of energy.

She tried to roll away from him and his hands and fingers found her breast. She gasped in a new agony of pain. The hand clamped over her mouth again. She tried to bite and he slapped her.

It was hard for her to breathe. She felt smothered. She relaxed for a moment and his hand loosened at her mouth. The other hand continued to explore her body, viciously hurting in its assault.

"Keep quiet," he commanded. "Shut up or I'll *really* hurt you."

She renewed her desperate struggle and he laughed and bore down with his weight as his mouth sought her skin. His fingers clawed and twisted and sank into the softness of her body. Her naked legs flailed as she tried to escape from him. Her fists beat at him.

Girls had been seriously injured by men like this. Girls had gone to hospitals, torn, bruised, broken by a sadism that could become maniacal. And for some girls it was not a hospital bed, but the sterile coldness of the morgue.

She had to get away from this man. She had to get off this bed and away from this man and out of this room. This was something she could not control, a man she couldn't handle. This could be death.

Now he was kneeling over her, his hand methodically slapping her. She tried to scream and the hand covered her mouth again. A fist jarred against her jaw and she sank into darkness.

When she opened her eyes again she was lying on the bed. She knew that, and she knew, also that she literally had been raped. Her insides felt bruised and torn.

She tried to move a hand down but she couldn't. She realized that her hands were tied above her head. She couldn't move her legs. Something was across her mouth and she had to breathe through her nose. She looked up into the man's face. He wore the intense, harsh look. The lust look. He saw that she had regained consciousness and he nodded in satisfaction.

He moved away from her and when he returned he carried a leather belt in one hand. He whipped it up and down in a quick, slashing movement. Ann screamed against the gag and strained at the bindings on her arms and legs as pain burned across her bare abdomen. The belt slashed again, lower, and she thought she would faint.

An hour later the man held her upright with a hand clamped on her arm as they went down in the elevator. The operator was sleepy and not too curious.

"We'll take a walk, baby," the man said to Ann. "Those drinks were too stiff. All you need is fresh air." Obviously the words were for the operator's ears. He seemed indifferent.

Ann didn't answer. The pain inside was deep and violent. She wanted to be out of this elevator, out of the hotel, rid of this man—this beast. She wanted to be home. The pain was so violent and deep.

They were out in the street and the man was putting her in a taxi.

"Give him your address, baby," the man was saying.

She spoke it in a choked voice. The cab driver nodded. The man gave the driver a bill and stepped back and closed the taxi door.

It was a short ride. She got out of the taxi and went into her apartment house and to her apartment. She unlocked the door and closed it behind her. She dropped her handbag on the floor, the apartment key beside it. Then she couldn't stand any longer.

Slowly, almost desperately, she knelt and fell forward so that she was on her hands and knees. She began to crawl toward her bathroom. Liquid was dripping from her mouth. Dazedly she thought it was saliva. Or maybe she was nauseated.

She had forgotten to turn out the bathroom light when she had left earlier, and she crawled toward the shaft of light that came from the open doorway.

She crawled across the threshold and onto the cold white tile of the bathroom floor. Liquid still dripped from her mouth, although she swallowed frantically and tried to hold it back.

Suddenly she stopped crawling and looked down at the white tile, focusing her eyes against her dizziness and weakness.

The liquid made a small pool where she stopped. It slowly spread as the liquid dripped from her mouth. The liquid looked dark and soft.

"It's blood," she thought. "It's my blood."

Then she crumpled face down and the liquid continued to flow from her open mouth where her lips were loose against the tile....

CHAPTER ONE

O n Monday of that week, Ann Freeman had felt no premoni-
tion about the weekend. It was a singularly routine Monday
from the hour when she awoke shortly after noon.

Although she had carefully bathed after coming home, just
before two o'clock in the morning, she immediately battled again
as soon as she arose. Sometimes she bathed four and five times
a day.

When she came out of the bathroom she put several records
on a high fidelity player and fixed orange juice, coffee, and toast
for a quick breakfast. She read a contemporary novel while she
ate. She liked to read and the bookcase in her living room was
well filled.

After finishing her breakfast she washed the dishes and then
called the small and rather questionable answering service that
catered to girls "in the life" and others on the fringe areas of
society.

There was a call for her. She told the service that she would
accept other calls for a while and then dialed the number they
had given her. She asked to speak to Mr. Morrin and was put
through to him. His voice was hurried and slightly rasping.

"This is Ann Freeman, Mr. Morrin."

"Oh, yes, Ann. I left a call for you. I've an out-of-town customer here tonight."

"I'd like to meet him, Mr. Morrin."

"Fine, fine. The usual arrangements?"

"Of course."

"I'm certain you'll be interested in his line. Say at eight? The usual hotel. He has a suite—seven-ten."

"Mr. Smith?"

"As good a name as any," Mr. Morrin was inclined to be nervous and apprehensive. He preferred to cloak his transactions with her in a rather transparent double talk. Once he had asked her if she thought her telephone was tapped. She had assured him that it wasn't, but he still liked to talk in ambiguities.

Actually, many of the girls talked their own special kind of double talk in dealing with customers. Sometimes Ann wondered why men and women went to such great lengths negotiating their most fundamental mutual physical relationship. Even courtship and marriage—the legitimate negotiation—followed certain rules and regulations.

"I'll be there," Ann said. She knew that she would receive an envelope enclosing fifty dollars in the mail within a day or so. That was her arrangement with Mr. Morrin.

She hung up and returned to her bedroom and made up her bed. For a few moments she thought about going shopping for an hour or so, but decided against it. It was just possible that Mr. Bien might have had a bad weekend with his wife. If he had, he would want a "matinee" a little after four o'clock, after he had left his executive suite downtown.

She was fond of Carl Blen. Months before, after he had first gone to bed with her, he had insisted that she was underpaid.

"Ann, you're a hundred-dollar girl. I'm paying you that, whether you ask for it or not. It's worth more than that to me."

A few others paid a hundred dollars, and on certain occasions she set her price at that fee. Usually, however, she charged the fifty dollars. There were more customers to be found for that fee, and it was easier to find them.

She placed more records on the player. It was a strange selection. She didn't try to account for her tastes in music. If she liked Mancini and television background music, Tchaikovsky and ballet, Mahler and symphony in the same stack on the record spindle, it only reflected what she liked to consider a cosmopolitan taste that she had developed in her young life.

Or, perhaps it went with the three years of university classes, the brief excursion into theatricals, modeling, TV, and the smart men she had known. It might even reflect the large, rambling home in Missoula where she had grown up; and possibly Casey Shean, the wild Irish boy from Butte who had attended the university and rented a room in an old house.

Yes, it might certainly reflect him because he also had a stack of records such as these, and in the semi-darkness of a single small gooseneck lamp bent very low over a desk across the room from the day bed, they had often listened to the music turned low so that the landlady would not be disturbed.

This also was the way the sex part had begun back in Montana. Suddenly the memory of those days was very vivid and she recalled how she would lie in bed and turn her head on the pillow so that she could see the strong, Irish profile, the unruly curl of hair, the twisted smile of Casey's lips while she luxuriated in the warm cushion of his arm beneath her neck, the muscular hardness of his body beside her.

He had a ruggedness of features that bespoke strength and toughness and gentleness. He was not handsome by the standards of Hollywood, or a magazine ad or TV commercial, but he had a strong masculine definition of features, with the long nose, firm chin, wide-spread eyes, and strong white teeth. Women would always be attracted to him.

Moments before, she had traced his profile with one finger and then he had stopped her with a fast, hard embrace and rough lips that were demanding. He had released her as suddenly as he had held her.

"A woman is made to be loved by a man," he said softly, almost reverently. "Look at you! Look at what a woman you are!"

She watched him smile at her as he lay on one side, gazing into her face that was turned toward him. She saw his eyes leave their inspection of her eyes and nose and lips and concentrate for a second on her throat, and then upon her covered breasts so that she was almost uncomfortably aware of their upthrusting fullness and strange hardening of her nipples.

He reached out a hand to follow his gaze. She felt its touch and pressure and demand and she knew that a blush was on her throat and cheeks. She closed her eyes.

She felt his other hand at the hemline of her skirt, and then the fast, quick caress along the inner smoothness of her thighs.

His movements were careful and certain. She trembled and her eyes opened wide. She saw new intentness in his expression, his slightly parted lips. She heard his accelerated breathing. He smiled, confidently and possessively.

"Please, Casey," she whispered, reaching for his hands. "Don't ... don't touch me ..."

Her own hand was arrested in movement as she felt new awakenings in her body and fell victim to her own moment of intense sensation.

He bent his head over her so that he was large in her eyes. She felt his breath upon her cheeks and face. His lips were hard upon her mouth.

"You're soft and smooth and sweet," he murmured. "Your skin is velvet like rose petals. You're lovely. I love you ..."

Vainly she tried to lift her hands, but somehow her arms were gently pinioned by his arms and body. His hands were upon her, and she was conscious of a tremendous weakness, born of a strange warmth.

"I can't—we mustn't," she whispered, not meaning the words, yet desperately wanting to mean them because she was suddenly so helplessly and hopelessly frightened. "Please stop, Casey—please."

His mouth covered hers and she felt her lips loosen and open to him. He drew away and whispered.

"I'll roll up the sweater ... like this ... now, unfasten behind ... there ... ah, there! You're firm, darling. You're beautiful!"

"Oh, Casey ... please not ... don't kiss me like that ... not there. I can't stand it ... your hands ... don't ... oh, don't ... don't ... don't ..."

Certainly she had tried to stop him, not really wanting to stop him, but vaguely remembering her quiet and tired merchant father, and her mother's ambiguous warnings about "boys" and what she had learned from classes in the university. Certainly she was intelligent. Certainly she understood the mechanics of sex. She understood enough to know that she probably was safe from pregnancy because she was within a day or so of her menstrual period. She knew enough to know that Casey was talking with an Irish tongue and a hotness of blood and sexual intention.

The music stopped for seconds and another record clicked into place and the beat of Ravel's *Bolero* blended into the beat of her own pulse.

She struggled two times: the first time as he took the sweater over her head and kissed her bare shoulders and breasts until she was submissive; the second time when his fingers found the elastic band around her waist and pulled down swiftly and surely. This last was a long and desperate struggle because she was frightened, even as she knew that she would surrender—or because she knew.

She spoke only the words, "Please ... don't ... oh, please ..."
He said only, "I love you ... don't stop me ... I love you ..."

Then his weight was heavy on her, his hand fumbled between them, and she uttered her last instinctive protest. "No! No, Casey, no ..."

The pain of defloration was sharp. She cried out. She felt captured, assaulted, and wounded in the hard clasp of his arms and the demanding roughness of his mouth. Instinctively her hands clutched at him. She lifted her body in a convulsive, desperate, and futile effort to escape, and the movement only served to complete the male conquest.

Then, because there was nothing left for her to do, she accepted his love-making, hardly moving, trying to feel sensation and to realize what was happening.

She felt no delight. She experienced no soaring heights of passion. Even the excitement that had preceded this frantic activity was gone. She felt only a sensation of pain, and then soreness, and an unutterable feeling of violation. When it was all over, she opened her eyes and looked into his strained face, heard the elation of his voice when he spoke her name, and felt the full expenditure of his strength. But she experienced no pleasure.

That was the first time.

Afterwards she wept quietly in the small room, and listened to the monotone of his words.

"Believe me, darling," he said, "I love you. It's all right. I'm sorry. Terribly sorry. I can't tell you ... only I love you. I couldn't stop. I'm sorry ... but I couldn't stop."

He began to caress her again, almost tentatively, and he talked about her loveliness and what he called her beauty. He wiped tears from her cheeks with a forefinger, and he kissed her wet eyes. His unruly hair had fallen over his forehead, and there was the glisten of perspiration upon his skin. He had the odor of a man about him; not the unpleasant odor of uncleanliness, but the masculine odor of good health and youth and vigor.

She was quiet at his side, unresponsive, and a little chilly. The record player had finished the last record of the stack. The mechanism had clicked off, but the amplifier still was on and the warning light gleamed. Outside, a winter wind tore at the corners of the old, two-story rooming house. She would have to leave soon.

"Will I be pregnant?" she asked abruptly.

His caressing hand stopped and she felt the sudden tightening of his body. She saw the tenseness come into his broad, flat shoulders, and the quick uplift of his well-formed head, like an animal scenting danger. His profile was outlined briefly as he turned to look directly into her face. There, in his eyes, she saw a concern that was more boy than man.

"I didn't use anything," he said. "I'm sorry."

"Don't be sorry about anything more. You've already said you are sorry for so much. You had what you wanted and you liked it. I suppose you don't know if I'll be pregnant or not."

"Don't talk like that, Ann. You know how I feel about you."

"I know," she said. "You couldn't help it."

She remembered that she had thought about her probable safety from pregnancy before it had begun. Possibly she instinctively knew that it was going to happen, and she wondered if knowing that she probably was safe had made her allow it to happen. She might have stopped him if she really had wanted to stop him.

"I have to go home." She swung from the bed and picked up her plain, white rayon panties from the floor. A functional garment purchased from Penney's store at a modest price. Ordinary panties bought for everyday wear by a virgin attending the university. As she prepared to step into them she saw that she was bleeding slightly.

"Do you have some Kleenex, Casey?"

He got up from the bed. He had not removed his clothing and he had rearranged its disorder shortly after he had finished with her.

He found a box of cleansing tissues in a drawer and she used some to wipe away the blood and then to protect the undergarment. She dressed hurriedly, turning her back to him. He had lighted a cigarette and the smoke was strong in the small room. Finally she shrugged into her winter coat and was ready to leave.

"Are you going to drive me home?" she asked.

"Listen, Ann—" The Irish recklessness was gone now. He was a tall, young, uncomfortable, worried youth. "If you become pregnant—we'll be married, Ann. I promise you."

"It would be convenient," she smiled. "Come on, Casey. It's late."

Abruptly she realized how self-objective she could be. She felt strangely older. And looking at herself, and at what had happened, she thought: "So that's what it's like. Nothing. Really nothing."

Casey said, "You don't know how wonderful—"

"Please, Casey. We have to hurry."

An expression of doubt crossed his face.

"You act—almost as if it didn't mean anything," he said.

"Did it?" she asked. She opened the door and went out. The room was in the back of the old house and had its own outside door. The night was sharply cold and windy. Casey followed her, pulling the door shut after him and they walked along the side of the darkened house toward the street where his old car was parked.

"It's going to snow," Ann said.

"Ann, listen—I want you to know that I—"

She stopped so suddenly that he bumped into her. She turned to face him and she was as surprised by her sudden anger as he was.

"Will you please just skip it?" she demanded. "It happened, but nothing happened. Do I make it clear? Let's stop talking about it."

"Okay, then. Yeah—okay."

She turned again and walked briskly toward his car. As she opened the car door, not waiting for him to perform the courtesy, the first flakes of snow whirled with the wind.

Afterwards—in the warm security of her bed—she thought about everything that had happened during the night. She remembered the pain and the vigor of Casey's love-making. She had not experienced an orgasm and she knew it. There was no mystery for her about orgasm, but there was a disturbing worry that she had not experienced one with Casey in her first love-making with a man.

"Sometimes it doesn't happen," she assured herself. "I've read that in those books about marriage."

After a time she touched herself and she began to breathe more quickly. This was why she knew what an orgasm could be. She had long ago reassured herself that this was not abnormal. What did Hamilton report in the research in marriage that she had found in the library? Of a thousand college women, 60 percent of them had satisfied their sexual requirements in this manner at one time or another. By themselves. Probably in the warm quiet of their bedrooms and their beds. This overt expediency to achieve for her what—for tonight at least—a man had failed to do. To be among the 60 percent was not too bad. It couldn't be. She had plenty of company, she thought.

She let fantasy inspire a part of it tonight because of what had happened, but she revised the memory and the interval of love-making and finally abandoned the fantasy as she allowed herself the solitary luxury of self-satisfaction until she gasped softly in her release.

Now on a Monday afternoon she thought briefly of an evening nine years before.

"I was nineteen," she thought "Is that old or young to lose your virginity? Was it young then or old then? And now? What are girls of nineteen like today? After Kinsey reports and wars and all the furor about juvenile delinquency."

Well, young or old, that was how it had happened, and she had drifted into a brief but energetic affair with Casey Shean. There had been a great deal of sex because there was the opportunity—his room in the old house and a landlady who retired early and was almost deaf.

There was experimentation and the problem of contraception and one month of worry about a pregnancy that did not materialize.

If it all had happened now, they might have married. Kids in school married now. They married when they were in high school. A famous woman anthropologist had disturbing viewpoints about the young marriages.

But nine years ago Casey had said he would marry her if she became pregnant, and vaguely assumed that they might someday marry anyhow, but he had not urged it immediately, and neither had she, so they had not.

Instead they went to bed together and made love and experimented with erogenous zones and the gymnastics of love-making in the wild enthusiasm of youth.

Occasionally she experienced a semblance of orgasm as the various marriage manuals—borrowed by Casey on one pretext or another from a young married couple whom he knew—said she should. More frequently she did not.

All of this had occurred nine years before today, six years before she took her first money for going to bed with a man. And between the last time with Casey—on a cold spring night before the morning that he left for Butte at the end of the school term— and the first time for money, there had been a good many other men who had from her what Casey first had taken.

The last time with Casey—this was the one night that was to become a sharp, clear, significant memory to bring her frustrations, confound her hopes and nurture hate. This was the reminder that she could be completely a woman, even when nothing else over the years might reassure her again that she was.

They had gone to his room. His bags were packed, for he would leave early in the morning. The portable phonograph was closed because the records were packed. The pictures he had put on the walls were gone. The several pipes usually found on his desk were missing. His books were packed. It was almost the sterile room of vacancy.

But it was warm, and the desk light cast a soft and shaded light over the room. The day bed was intimately familiar. The blind was drawn, as usual. The same old, leather lounging chair once again held the skirt, panties, hose, garter belt, bra and sweater of the girl upon the day bed. And in the closet with its open door, Casey had neatly hung the clothes he had just removed from his own body.

This was the complete familiarity that they had achieved after the first time. This was the progress of love making that they had made: the delight in their nudity, the freedom for experimentation, and the desperate surrenders to passions they experienced.

Here, also, the refrain of Casey's anxious questions: "Did you, darling? Did you?"

And the small lie of her answer: "Yes ... yes." This untruth after she had learned that there would be, at the most, only a very slight experience of pleasure. It would be hardly more than a ripple of feeling.

Sometimes it seemed that she was outside herself, watching and appraising and evaluating, and know that it could not possibly be the climax that she read about. The semblance or orgasm—as she defined it to herself—that she occasionally experienced with Casey, in actuality failed to reach even the fulfillment that she might experience in the solitude of her own bed with her fantasies in self-caress.

Even this self-induced experience, she suspected, was a surface one. She had read that some women might experience two different culminations, one of a surface nature, and one of a deep and wholly satisfying nature far more profound than the other.

She knew that she never had experienced this second culmination, neither in her own excursions, nor in her love making with Casey.

At times she wondered if all women experienced these doubts and frustrations and desires—if all women thought as much about sex as she sometimes did.

Even beyond these doubts, frustrations and desires that she might be trying to resolve sexually with Casey, there were other frustrations and desires that were more vague and, possibly, deep-seated.

Years later she was to understand some of these disturbances through her natural cusiosity, her reading, and intense desire to know herself. She was to learn that the tight-lipped discipline and lack of warmth of her mother had engendered disturbances in the daughter. She was to learn that when she had sought security and love from her father and had found only a mild affection bordering upon indifference from that quiet, evasive, hen-pecked man—this, too, had left emotional scars upon her, things that she didn't realize until much later.

And most important to her adult comprehension years later, would be the memory of a conversation between her mother and father that she had heard one night when she was very young:

"Don't touch me. Don't come near me," the mother said tensely, her voice coming from the darkened bedroom across the hallway from Ann's small bedroom.

"But Alice—" Ann's father spoke in a pleading, almost whee-dling voice. *"It isn't natural, Alice. I'm a man and—"*

"A man! That's certainly the truth. And all you think about is one thing. Like all men. Ever!"

"But Alice—"

"And never care what happens to the woman. Making her pregnant. Making her go through that terrible pain: I never wanted children. You knew that. You deliberately gave me Ann!"

"It was an accident—I'm sorry."

"Sorry? And now you won't even take a hand in raising her. You leave everything to me. Well, you wanted Ann. Not me. Just remember that."

"Alice—it wasn't deliberate. I didn't want her. I knew how you felt about children."

"Stop talking about it. I'm going to sleep. Just remember that I'll do my duty and rear your child. But only because I feel a responsibility. You'll never get me pregnant again. I hated it! All of it! I didn't want her and I don't want another."

Years later this conversation—so vividly remembered—along with her tears of loneliness and the hurt of being unwanted, were to be interpreted into an explanation for Ann's desire to be loved by someone.

The constant quest for a father's love that her own father had failed to give her, and the unconscious desire for revenge against a mother who had resented her were strange, driving motivations for Ann.

To be loved; to be wanted; to be needed—desperately Ann had wanted these things more than anything else. Yet in her quest for all of this with Casey, she had been vaguely unsatisfied. She had no idea how far her quest would drive her; that it would be expressed in a measure of frigidity; that it would send her from man to man as she sought what psychiatrists might call the "father image"—that it would set the pattern of her life, as it had for many other girls who eventually entered "the oldest profession."

On this spring night as she lay on Casey's bed while he prepared to make love to her, she realized that in all probability this would be their last time. The realization came when she acknowledged to herself that she certainly was not in love with him as he apparently was with her.

Casey talked about their future together—vaguely, it was true—but still in terms of "Someday we'll ..." or "... when I get through school and we can ..."

Lately he had talked about her coming to Butte to visit during the summer, and he vaguely assumed, in this, too, that their relationship somehow would continue.

Of immediate concern to him was getting to Butte and a job that awaited him in a public utilities office. He talked about it now.

"It's a chance to get set, Ann. After some general work in several departments, I'll eventually try for sales. That's where I want to be."

He sat on the edge of the bed and looked down at her.

"God you're beautiful, Ann. There's no one like you."

"You've seen quite a few others?" she smiled, half teasing.

He grinned and shook his head. The shaded light made his body look tanned, and, in fact, there still remained a small definition of tan from the previous summer. He had a good breadth of shoulders, well-developed muscles across his chest and down his solid arms, legs and thighs. He had played football until an ankle injury had ended his athletic career. Ann enjoyed looking at him.

"Tell me, Casey," she persisted. "I never asked before. Have you seen other girls like this? Have you had many girls? What were they like?"

"You want the honest Irish truth?"

"Certainly!"

"I'll tell you. Three other girls. One was a high school girl in my class. She was the first. It wasn't very good. I was too eager. Then a married woman who lived near us. She was older than I was—a sort of tramp with a nice husband. She was pretty. It wasn't very good with her, either. I was afraid her husband would come home."

He shook his head a little and smiled. He put a tentative, caressing hand on her.

"The third?" she prompted.

"I'd better not. I don't think you'd like it."

"Why? It's all right. I want to know."

"A girl down on the line."

"You mean a prostitute?"

"Does that disgust you?"

"No. It makes me curious. Was she good, Casey?"

"Look, let's not talk about it."

"No, really, I want to know. Was she good?"

"Yes. Why shouldn't she be?"

"As good as I am?"

"That's a crazy question!"

"Tell me."

"No. She wasn't as good," he said, but his voice seemed to lack conviction and she smiled at the slight evasiveness in his eyes.

Suddenly, what had begun almost as idle curiosity about another woman who was a prostitute became an exciting interest. She wondered what it would be like to sell herself; to place herself completely in the hands of a man for money; to do as he told her; to submit to what he demanded for his money. She pictured Casey with another woman. She wondered what another woman could give Casey that she did not; how she could please Casey more than the prostitute obviously had.

The perverse trend of thought increased her excitement. She experienced a strange, compelling desire to surpass the prostitute in pleasing Casey.

"Is a professional different?" she asked, moving restlessly under Casey's hands so that he began to breathe more quickly.

"Listen, Ann, no woman's better than you."

"*She* was. She had more experience."

"Cut it out." His smile and tone of voice were obvious. He had had enough of the conversation.

"No. Let's talk about it. It's exciting. Tell me about it. What did she do? What did she say? How much did you pay her? How did she act?"

"You're a crazy kid," he grinned in resignation, obviously disturbed a little by her questions. "There isn't anything much to tell. I paid her and we went to bed and that was it."

"That wasn't all. How did she make love?"

"For God's sake, Ann! She just made love. Like a woman makes love."

"Like I do?"

"Well … maybe everyone is a little different."

"Then she did things I don't do?"

"Well … she responded. So do you. But—look, this is crazy talk. Let's drop it. Tonight's our last—"

Ann laughed softly and stretched luxuriously under his caressing hands, seeing his excitement for her increase, and enjoying it.

"Shall I be better than she was?" she asked softly.

"You are."

"No. She was experienced. But I could learn. Or maybe a woman knows instinctively. Shall I be your whore tonight, Casey? Shall I do things I've never done before?"

She rested her arms back over her head and offered him the free and unspoken invitation to her body. She shut her eyes and tried to imagine that she was selling herself to him. Bought and paid for and now she must give him his money's worth.

Her excitement was contagious. She felt his heavy breathing and there was a new and strange demand in his hands and arms and mouth. She was acutely aware of the feel of his muscled, male body as he crowded close to her.

"Call me that," she whispered, twisting against him. "Let's be crazy—let's pretend. Call me that!"

"Whore!" he said harshly. "Little hot whore!"

"Yes, yes, yes! And you're going to like me. I'll make you like me. Like this!"

Thus it began for the last time, and it was strange and new and perversely exciting for her. She felt new sensations come to life deep within her, and she lost consciousness of the room, and the dim lights and the faint sound of the day bed springs.

She heard the heavy rhythm of Casey's breathing, and the night became a new rhythm as she transcended the previous depths she had known. Her response became abandoned and wanton. She moaned. Her fingernails raked deep into the skin of his back, and suspense mounted to a breathless desperation that she had to break; that he must break for her. In a frenzy of motion she sought his deliverance of her.

Then it was upon her and for a second she was certain that it was a sweet death, and then it was a prolonged agony of sensation too exquisite to bear, and finally came the abandon of sweet relief pulsing in powerful waves through her body ...

Long afterwards she wept once again in his arms, and clung to him. When it was time to go he kissed her.

"No tears, Ann. Please. We have a lifetime before us."

"Yes," she whispered, knowing instinctively that she did not believe her reply, that they would not see one another during the summer, and that this was to end—at least for now.

Casey kissed her wet eyes. "Then why are you crying?"

"I don't know," she said.

How could she tell him that she wept because she finally had experienced the completeness only when it was the end? That she had shared with him the ultimate in physical communion only when it was the last with him? None of this could she explain to him. It was a private, personal moment that she must keep to herself.

Then she remembered the excitement and why it had happened, and she smiled to herself.

"Tell me, Casey," she whispered. "Would I make a good whore?"

"The best," he laughed softly. "The best. But only with me."

"Was the other girl better?"

"Truly, no," he said and swept her to him in another kiss. "You'd better go. It's after midnight."

And that was how it ended for them.

Sometimes the memories, such as these, crowded in upon her and left her in a deep depression. This was something that she knew would always be with her. Depression, she had learned, was one of the great burdens that call girls, prostitutes, mistresses, and most women without sanctified male security, had to endure.

She could feel it right now, on this Monday afternoon, as she thought about Casey and the long-gone years. She was glad when the telephone rang, and pleased to hear Carl Blen's voice.

"Four-thirty?" he asked.

"Yes."

"I'll have about an hour."

"We'll make good use of it!"

"I'm certain we will," he chuckled and hung up.

The day was starting well for her. These two dates meant $150, because Bien would give her more. Last week had been especially good. She had earned $700. That meant fourteen men; fourteen brief imitations of a woman in passion; fourteen satisfied customers fourteen acts of coitus from which she had experienced no sexual satisfaction, but from which fourteen men had obtained full satisfaction for their money.

If she could earn $700 every week, that would be $2100 for four weeks, counting one week out for her period. Perhaps there were some girls who managed to work the full four weeks, and certainly those who had undergone hysterectomies might do that, but she preferred not to work the better part of one week of the four. The business actually was so biological and functionally mundane in so many ways.

But she knew that she was dreaming if she planned $2100 income every four weeks. It wouldn't work out that way, even for a girl like herself who had no man to keep. She knew that some of the better call girls in New York might average $20,000 gross a year, but she also knew that it would be difficult for a girl to earn that in this West Coast city.

She poured another cup of coffee and mentally played with the financial figures. If she could average $2100 every four weeks, that would be thirteen times that amount for the year. Well, make it just $2000 every four weeks and that would be $26,000 for the year.

She wouldn't make that much, but she might earn $15,000. She never had kept accurate accounts of her earnings. She paid no income tax. She had never been questioned about taxes. She was seldom questioned about anything from people who lived on the truly legitimate side of life. Except for the customers—the "Johns".

The "Johns" always had a question. "How did a girl like you get into a life like this?" Stock question number one in any whorehouse or hotel bed temporarily occupied by a call girl. Men wanted to know.

And the girl could ask herself where the money went. She thought about her expenditures.

The apartment was expensive, three hundred dollars by the time she had tipped the desk man, the garage attendant, the janitor, and paid the woman who took care of heavy cleaning chores.

Laundry took money, especially if she entertained in the apartment. A man liked clean, fresh bed linen. Towels were so necessary.

Clothing. Only expensive clothing. A girl had to look expensive if she was a hundred-dollar or a fifty-dollar girl. She had to have expensive, smart clothes; clothes such as few of the wives would—or could—afford.

There was Marcel, the hairdresser with the obvious name. He was expensive and everyone in his shop was expensive and they all expected large tips. But a girl came out of Marcel's place looking expensive, exclusive, and desirable.

There was the quiet, middle-aged doctor who sent his regular monthly bills for routine examinations and occasionally treatment of one sort or other.

Another doctor, who practiced in an unassuming office in an old building, also had received money from her. He charged $300 for an abortion.

Downtown was a savings account with three thousand dollars in it. This was for emergencies. Trouble with the police could bring about such an emergency. A certain attorney also had access to that fund. She had thought of this particular arrangement. Usually a girl had her man to take care of such problems.

In the basement garage of the apartment building was her fairly new convertible. It had cost her about $4,000.

In one of her closets was a mink coat. She had bought a new one each of the three years that she had been in "the life."

Ann also had another bank account that she guarded so carefully that she almost kept it a secret from herself. Religiously she placed money in it, keeping the passbook well hidden in her apartment, and never confusing the savings with her emergency savings. This was the money she called her "up-and-beyond" money. The phrase didn't mean anything except in the simplicity of its own definition.

If she had a man the money would certainly have been his, and most of the girls whom Ann knew "in the life" had such men. The kept men. Not the procurers, because there was a difference between a girl's kept pimp and a procurer. These kept men were the symbols of the girls' earning abilities.

In a brash and unusual outbreak of honesty, Sally Smith—the first call girl Ann had ever known—had explained the man she was currently supporting.

"He's sort of a status symbol, like they talk about in advertising," she said. "One of my customers is an advertising man. He was telling me about status symbols once. That's what Jack is to me. A status symbol. He drives a Cad that I bought him. He wears three-hundred-dollar suits. His shirts are custom-made. His shoes. Everything. And all of it from what I earn on my back for him. He's lower than I am, really, but I keep him in style. I'm a hundred-dollar girl and he proves it!"

In the months and years that followed, Ann was to remember Sally's observation. And perhaps because she remembered Sally's broken, bruised face after Jack had beaten her, she had carefully avoided any alliance with a man. Even when Sally had excused her "status symbol" by explaining his heavy drinking and uncontrollable anger, Ann had shuddered and resolved to conduct her own business.

Quietly and carefully she had learned the techniques of getting business, of avoiding trouble, and of preparing for trouble if it came.

A few other girls who worked alone, and some of the lesbians—who disdained any association with a man, other than for strictly business purposes—had taught her essentials.

In three years she had built a small but profitable business for herself. The answering service (another $50 a month) was a great help. Her associations with businessmen who needed party girls had become profitable. Her regulars were faithful. And the secret bank account was slowly, steadily building.

She refused to think about income taxes—she knew businessmen who avoided paying them as much as possible in devious and unethical ways. Maybe it was a reflection upon the great immorality some people thought was sweeping the nation. But she couldn't visualize herself as filling out a tax form and writing "call girl" as her employment. Anyhow—so what? It was a way of life. She didn't make the world. She only lived in it; as best she could.

The coffee cup was empty again.

"Skip the thinking," she admonished herself. "You'll think yourself real deep into the blues. Real, real deep."

She flipped through a stack of records and put on Mancini's Mr. Lucky music. This was music that gave her a lift, except that it disturbed her a little because it made her think of television and the few parts she had managed to get that year before she went to bed the first time for money.

Her door chime sounded and she knew it would be the cleaning woman. This was a Monday, Wednesday and Friday arrangement, between one-thirty and three.

She opened the door for a middle-aged Negro woman who smiled broadly.

"Good afternoon, Miss Freeman."

"There isn't much to do, Minnie."

"You want I should hurry?"

"Not necessarily. There just isn't much. Make the bed—change the linen. I ate out last night and there aren't any dishes. Vacuum and dust."

"There never is very much, Miss Freeman."

Ann was fairly certain that Minnie knew exactly how her part-time employer earned a living, and she was just as certain that Minnie was not concerned about it, nor particularly critical.

While Minnie worked in the bedroom, Ann returned to the bathroom and used cosmetics. She dressed in a new lounging set that she had purchased the week before. She wore nothing under the soft, clinging material. The trousers were closefitting at the waist and over her long, curved thighs. The top accented the firm, pleasing lines of her body. Carl Blen would approve.

She picked up her book and read while Minnie worked. She thought that she should have dressed and gone out for a while, but four-thirty was not too far away and the book was good. Furthermore, she was lazy and a little tired, with a full day before her.

Minnie had left and she was still reading when she realized that it was four o'clock. The phone had not rung again. She went to it and told the answering service to take her calls. Then she went to the bedroom and turned back the covers and sheet on the bed.

In the kitchen she made certain that there was Scotch and soda. Blen always liked a drink when he came straight from the office. She made certain that there were plenty of large bath towels in the bathroom. He probably would want to take a quick shower. She quickly and deftly put a contraceptive diaphragm in place before she left the bathroom.

She opened a closet door that held a full-length mirror and inspected herself in the lounging clothes, debating whether or not to change. She decided that she had been right—Mr. Blen would approve. She placed a discreet amount of perfume at strategic places on her body, and then selected records with care. Blen liked what he called "walkaround" music.

"The kind you background models in a fashion show with," he explained. "Good for love making, too."

Mr. Blen made a small production of everything, including the love making that he bought.

She was ready for him when the chime sounded again and she let him in.

He was tall and thin and definitely middle-aged. His suit was conservatively cut. His shirt was expensive. His sandy hair was heavily grayed. He had acquired a golf tan that he wore attractively.

Ann smiled at him with genuine liking. They had become friends in a singularly unorthodox manner. Once in a while he talked about his business and his past and more infrequently about his wife.

"I married a bitch," he said ruefully one night after they had finished their love making. "It was one of those good marriages. Her family knew my family. We grew up in the same neighborhood. Went to the same schools. Approved by the same people. I didn't know she was alive as a woman until I was twenty-two and just out of college. We went on a date—just a casual country club sort of thing. Only it was a little more to her. It was the beginning of a campaign.

"She had it figured out to the last decimal point right from the beginning. She knew I would be in a paying business—my family owned it. She knew all there was to know about me. My sisters were her friends. My mother was her mother's friend. Our fathers probably had a couple of drinks in the locker room at the club and agreed that it was a good idea one of these days if it worked out that way. And it did. Boy! It did!"

"How do you mean?"

He laughed quietly and took time to light a cigarette from the pack at her bedside.

"I finally woke up to what was happening and I didn't want any part of it. She had looks and position and even some money of her own. She had a lot of things, but she didn't have what I really wanted."

"But she got you."

"She got me. A war came along. I enlisted. Do you know how she got me? Right when I thought I had the perfect out? When I thought I'd get away to war and things would work out so I could skip marrying her and find what I really wanted? Know how?"

"I have an idea. I'm sort of in the business, you know."

"And you're so right. The night before I left for training camp we went out and had some drinks and we parked. Get this, Ann. Parked like a couple of high school kids out by the country club. And that quiet, well-reared, highly educated, impeccably proper little bitch really went to work on me. The next day I had a terrific guilt complex until I remembered something."

"What did you remember?"

"That I didn't have to take off her pants—or even ask her to. She suggested it herself and did it herself. She took the lead in all of it. Maybe I thought I was scoring big, as the saying goes these days, but I wasn't. She was. So when I got a three-day pass a couple of weeks later and flew home, she told me that she thought she was pregnant and we had our quick little war marriage."

"And was she?"

"Pregnant?"

"Yes."

"No."

Other segments of the story came later, including the accurate description of the frigid wife and the calculating spouse. So had grown their friendship to this afternoon and Carl Blen admiring her lounging set.

"New?" he asked.

"The first time I've worn it."

"Sexy, too."

"Well? Isn't that the idea?"

He laughed. "My wife would have frozen at the suggestion. But then, she wouldn't wear anything like that. Even if she still has the figure for it."

"She's pretty?"

"For middle age, yes. She spends a great deal of time making certain that she is. She's proud of her size twelve, and her lack of obvious wrinkles. She evidently thinks that sex isn't good for all that."

"Narcissistic?"

He looked at her with a slight expression of surprise.

"Narcissism goes hand in hand with frigidity sometimes," she said.

"I didn't know you dabbled in psychiatry."

"I read a lot. Sex is my business, so naturally I read about it, along with eveything else."

"How about other girls? Do they read as much as you do?"

"Some don't read at all, but quite a few do. I know some girls who are even intellectuals."

He looked a little skeptical. For a fraction of a second a flash of resentment flashed into her eyes, despite her natural liking for the man.

"Don't misunderstand me," she said. "Or *us*. I'm not an ordinary prostitute—a street girl or a house girl. Don't get the idea that I—"

"I don't," he interrupted smiling. She immediately regretted the anger in her voice. She hadn't meant to be obvious. He was a good customer, and even a friend, in a manner of speaking, and she had no reason to defend herself or to be angry with him. As a matter of fact, he thought so highly of her professional services that he doubled the fee she usually received. Of course, he could well afford it, and that made a difference, she supposed.

"I'll get your drink," she said with a slightly guilty smile. "So I sometimes read Caprio and Karpman and even Krafft-Ebing—a friend loaned me the book and I got interested."

"A customer?"

She shook her head. "A lesbian. Maybe she wanted to prove a point." Ann laughed and turned away and went to the kitchen. She brought back two drinks.

He sampled his and nodded approvingly as he sprawled comfortably in a low, Swedish modern chair. "I never thought about it," he said thoughtfully, "but I suppose you have different—classifications? Categories? What would you call them?"

Ann shrugged again. "Categories, maybe. I don't know. But there are differences. Not everyone agrees, but I think there's a kind of basic difference all the way down the line."

"Like?"

"Well, I'm a call girl. I work by appointment, as you know. Then there are street girls, and there are house girls—and party girls, if you want to count them."

"Oh?"

"Party girls like to rationalize what they're doing by reserving the right to turn down a date. But when they take one—and it's almost always only one for the night—the money they take is the same kind that we do."

"And there are fifty-dollar girls and hundred-dollar girls," he said from his own knowledge.

"Right. So you see I didn't have to explain so much. And you've finished your drink. There's a zipper on the top of this thing. Would you like to unzip for me?"

She went to his chair and turned so that he could reach the zipper.

"It's a pleasure," he said. "A real pleasure!"

A few moments later she stretched out lazily on her bed, nude and relaxed, as she idly watched Carl Blen undress.

Her workday was about to begin.

CHAPTER TWO

She had dinner at a quiet restaurant where she frequently ate. Carl Blen had left shortly after six o'clock, leaving his customary hundred dollars in crisp, new twenty-dollar bills. He had even kissed her good bye, and she had accepted the kiss—something she seldom encouraged from customers.

Occasionally she wondered about the strange reluctance to kiss a man who had bought her, even while she performed the ultimate act of intimacy with him. Other girls felt the same way about it. A kiss was still a private, personal thing. To an even greater extent, the clinically described female orgasm was solely a personal and private experience that a girl like Ann preferred to share only on occasion and specifically with a person with whom she wished to share it.

There were so many masculine misconceptions about prostitutes; so many beliefs that were carefully built up and nurtured to feed a man's vanity along with his sexual desires.

The misconceptions were important for good business. A smart girl always simulated a climactic response to accompany the man's. He had to believe that he was good. Men wanted to think they were superb in bed. Ann suspected that women wanted to think they were equally good. Possibly this was a universal desire—to be good in bed. Yet—Ann thought—so few were!

She was drinking a second cup of coffee when Clara Lindy came in. She had an apartment two floors above Ann's and prided herself upon being a "strictly hundred-dollar girl." She was tall and black-haired and looked as if she certainly belonged on the stage, in motion pictures, or on a television screen. Her stock in trade was glamor, and she carefully cultivated it.

She sat at the table with Ann and ordered coffee. She was frowning and appeared to be dejected.

"Low?" Ann asked.

Clara lit a cigarette and nodded disconsolately. "Mike. Honestly, Ann, sometimes he simply bugs me. You know? Like I could use a razor blade on my wrist, or something?"

Ann nodded. Clara had been keeping Mike Lane for almost a year. She had kept him too well. There was the Cadillac convertible, and the expensive suits, and the money he spent in the "beat" joints where he liked to be seen with his fellow pimps. His was the language that Clara used when she was with her own: his language, his desires, extravagances, demands, ill temper, and undeniable good looks were hers.

"Something new?"

"He's using horse. Not that I don't understand. But do you know what it costs to buy him his drugs every day? That nice, expensive heroin? Have you any idea?"

"I've heard what it costs."

"Ann, you know I treat him well. Who else treats a man better? But now he's on the kick. It started easy and I didn't know until last week, and now he's hooked."

"You've problems, honey."

"More than that. He—" she hesitated a few seconds. "Ann, tell me something. We've been friends a long time, haven't we?"

"A long time, Clara. What do you want to know?"

"Has he talked to you? I mean—has he asked you ...?"

Ann shook her head, feeling a quick pity for Clara. Obviously Mike had threatened to add another girl or two to build a stable. She knew how Clara would feel about a "wife-in-law" and she was glad that she could say that Mike hadn't propositioned her.

"You know how I feel, Ann," Clara continued. "Not that I probably couldn't do better than Mike. Only—well, I'm damned used to him."

Clara crushed out her cigarette and almost immediately lit another. "He's supposed to meet me here for dinner. Don't say anything."

"Of course not."

"If you had a man, you'd understand."

"I understand without having one," Ann nodded. "Here he comes. Who's with him?"

"Cal Marker. Don't you know him?"

Ann shook her head and continued to look at the two men approaching the table. She already had dismissed the sharply dressed Mike. She knew him only too well. But she was interested in his companion.

Cal Marker appeared to be in his late twenties or early thirties. He was of medium height and build and was hatless. His hair was cut short and close, compatible with his Ivy League clothing, his smooth mannerisms and tolerant smile.

"What is he?" Ann asked softly. "A college prof, advertising man, junior executive, or clothing salesman?"

Clara managed a tired smile. "Darling, he's just another pimp. But he *is* different. And he has three girls."

"I'll bet they've bought him a Jag to drive."

"*And* a Thunderbird."

The two men joined them and introductions were made. Cal Marker gave Clara a casual greeting and immediately devoted his attention to Ann.

"Well!" he smiled. "You're new."

"Not that new," Ann replied. He had cool green eyes and his teeth were very white. Everything about him was in good taste. She was certain the English tab collar shirt was imported. The material of his suit and the tailoring could only have come from a custom tailor.

He glanced at Clara and Mike. "You never told me about her," he accused.

Mike shrugged and motioned for a waiter. "Clara's best friend," he said, looking bored. "I thought you knew each other."

"Oh?" Marker said, with a knowing note in the word as if Mike's explanation had been more detailed. He looked at Clara and then at Ann.

Ann smiled and nodded. "I'm one of the girls. You can talk freely."

"Strange," he murmured. "No one's ever mentioned you."

"None of your playmates would," she said. "I mean the guys. I don't have one. And I don't want one."

He quizzically lifted an eyebrow. He did it rather well, she thought. Now he looked more and more like a smart young guy from a smart private eye show on TV. She almost expected a little progressive jazz background. One thing for sure—she thought in the vernacular of her company—not one square in a thousand would ever dig him for what he was.

"Let's talk about it sometime," he said. "Maybe you need a guy."

"You couldn't get me anything I don't have, and I'd have a lot less having you."

"You'd have someone to look after you."

"I hear you already have a Jag and a Thunderbird. Do you want to add a Mercedes or a Porshe to your garage?"

"Maybe I'd just like to add you to my stable," he grinned.

"I'm going to end up disliking you," Ann told him, not entirely in repartee. Across their own corner of the table Clara and Mike were in a low-voiced, vicious argument.

Suddenly Clara stood and angrily left the table. Mike watched her walk away and after a moment he followed her. Ann and Cal Marker looked at one another.

"Now just what would your remedy be?" Ann asked icily. "A beating. It'll probably be Mike's."

"I don't beat my women," Marker smiled tightly. "They don't act that way."

"Well, dig *him*!"

"Let's play it straight for a minute," Marker said, his smile still tight, but his eyes narrowing a little. "Let's talk it over. I can offer quite a bit."

"You can offer like nothing."

"Let's look at the fringe benefits first."

"You don't have to talk like a junior executive just because you dress like one."

He disregarded her caustic voice and continued to speak quietly: "You'll have someone to take care of bail, if you need it. Someone to look after those details. Someone to help now and then in lining up something really big. Someone to look to if you get in trouble."

"Someone to give the money I earn," she said shortly. "And what do I really get for my money? You? Do I get to sleep one night a week with you? Do I get to help buy you more cars and more suits and give you the chance to spend it big with the other guys like you?"

"My, my, aren't we bitter!" He continued to smile, and his voice and words were not what she had learned to expect from men like him. His eyes had narrowed even more, and there was a depth of anger and cruelty in them that she distinctly recognized now.

Abruptly she was impatient with herself because she realized that she also feared this man, and even in the fear, she recognized his significance to her. She understood why he had a stable of girls, and understanding made her fear a little for herself. She was vulnerable. Now she knew it.

"I've got to go," she said and reached for her check the waiter had just left. Marker's hand closed over hers. He took the check, deftly, as if he made a practice of paying checks with the money he obtained from his women.

"Think about it," he said. "We could do worse. Both of us."

"I've already thought about it. Good night."

She got up and hurriedly left the restaurant. She glanced automatically at her watch. It still was early. Possibly there were messages for her at the answering service. She found a pay telephone and called. There were no messages.

She already had earned one hundred dollars, and there would be another fifty from the hotel date later. She had the choice of returning to her apartment, or of going to a movie. She decided upon the movie.

The picture bored her, or perhaps, she admitted, she found that Cal Marker was insinuating himself into her mind to the point where she couldn't keep her attention focused on the broad screen before her.

Idly she wondered about the girls who kept him, and why they did, and how he treated them. What was it besides the status symbol? Was it loneliness, too? Was it wanting someone to depend upon, or who depended upon you? Was it the chance to go to bed with a man you were buying rather than a man who was buying you? Was that really it? A sort of revenge against all the men who bought you and used you? So you could say to yourself, "Now I'll buy me a man. And I'll use him. Bought and paid for! Lower than I am. Lower, lower, lower than I am! A man who is lower than a whore!"

She shut her eyes in the theater and tried to think of something else. This was the kind of thinking that was bad. She mustn't think this way. She had better leave the theater. It was getting close to eight o'clock and she had the hotel date. She had to go to work.

She left the theater and window-shopped until a few moments before eight. She took a taxi to the hotel and went directly to suite 710. A middle-aged man nervously let her in.

"Mr. Morrin said you'd be here," he said. "Er ... my name's Smith."

Obviously this was not an ordinary experience for him. She wondered if he had suggested the interlude, or if Mr. Morrin had. She suspected that Mr. Morrin had. He was the seller. "Mr. Smith" was the buyer. Possibly an influential one. And Mr. Morrin was using a sales aid to get his pitch across.

She looked more closely at her customer. He was getting a little paunchy. His hair showed gray at the temples. A fraternal ring was on one hand. He wore the jacket to his business suit.

He was too fussed to ask her to sit down, so she crossed the room and sat in a low chair by a coffee table in the small living room.

"Oh, yes," the man stammered. "Sit down ... I mean ... well! I suppose you'd like a drink, Miss ... Miss ... ?"

"Miss Freeman—Ann," she smiled. "I won't need the drink, unless you'd particularly like to have one, Mr. Smith."

Suddenly he smiled, and some of the nervousness seemed to disappear.

"I'm not Smith. That was Morrin's idea. I suppose you could easily find out my name if you liked, and I don't suppose it matters much if you know it or not. Morrin assures me the hotel people won't bother us."

"I'm certain they won't."

"Good. Actually my name is almost as common as Smith. It's plain Jones—Harry Jones. I run an out-of-town business and I'm buying quite a bit of stuff from Morrin. He suggested over drinks last night that I might like to have a little company tonight. And—well, the idea appealed to me."

"I'm glad of that," Ann smiled. She knew from experience that this could be a quick trick because he would be nervous, a little frightened, and probably was indulging in adultery for the first time in years—even possibly for the first time in a long married life. He probably would need a little help in resolving the purpose of her visit. Her implied compliment that she was glad he had decided to accept Morrin's offer would help.

"I'm hardly a movie star," he grinned. "Fifty and getting a little fat."

She shook her head. "Mature, Mr. Jones. There's a difference. I like mature men."

He obviously was flattered.

"I still think a girl as nice-looking as you would prefer some-one younger."

"And inexperienced?" she asked with a knowing glance. "A girl wants to know that she's being loved by a man. A real man—not a boy."

Harry Jones liked what he heard. He lost all evidences of nervousness as he nodded sagely. "I suppose so," he said. "I remember when I was younger. Impatient. Always in a hurry."

And you probably will be tonight, Ann thought. *Or you'll be so excited you won't be able to perform at all. But I'll help you, Mr. Jones. I'll earn my fifty dollars and make you happy. You and Mr. Morrin.*

Hiding her slight amusement she watched her customer try to maneuver the transaction into a more active stage. He glanced toward the bedroom door and back at her. He mixed a small quick drink for himself, accepting her refusal again. He drank it hurriedly.

"Well ... ?" he said tentatively.

Ann got up and said, "I'm going to enjoy this, Mr. Jones. Truly."

She walked into the bedroom and waited for him to come in. He had put down his drink and there was moisture on his forehead from renewed nervousness. Obviously he was no old hand at the processes of fornication with a call girl in a hotel room.

"Your coat," Ann smiled, as if she were a housewife welcoming a guest into her home. She took it casually from him and hung it up in a closet. He stood and watched her. She returned to him and untied his necktie, flirting outrageously with him as she accomplished the small task and moving slightly against him. She took the necktie from around his neck and put it on the top of the dressing table.

Then standing slightly across the room from him, she smiled, almost secretly, and unfastened the light cotton skirt she wore. She stepped out of it, knowing that the half slip she wore was even more attractive than the skirt.

She unbuttoned her blouse and slipped out of it, knowing that he would be intrigued by the expensive and thin brassiere over the full pertness of her breasts. She waited a moment and then went to him and turned.

"Unfasten?" she asked.

His fingers fumbled at the relatively simple brassiere fastening. It came loose and he took it from her. His hands closed over her bare breasts until she gently removed them and turned and came close against him.

He tried to kiss her, but she deftly avoided his mouth on hers so that his lips crushed against a cheek. She moved against him tantalizingly and was conscious of his masculine readiness.

Again she moved back from him and stepped out of the half-slip. She wore no hose or garter belt, and the single undergarment that she wore was expensively designed for allure and flattery.

"You'd better undress," she said softly. "I don't want to wait any longer."

I could wait all night, she thought, *and still feel as indifferent as I do at this moment. But I'm paid to be excited and eager. I'll give you a good imitation for the money, Mr. Jones.*

8:25 P.M.

"Say ... I'm sorry, Ann. I mean ..."

"It happens to every man now and then. Don't worry about it."

"Usually—"

"You don't have to explain. Why don't we rest for a few moments?"

"I suppose we could."

"Certainly. There. Relax. We have plenty of time."

"But don't you work on a one-time basis, or—I mean, isn't once all you're supposed to—?"

"Some girls do and some don't. We have time, and it was really sort of an accident for you."

"I suppose there's a ... fee? That Morrin pays? He implied that. Couldn't I increase it if you'd stay awhile?"

"Then you really don't want me to leave?"

"I want you to stay."

"A lot of men would be urging me to get dressed and out by now. Why don't you just rest and relax? Let me take care of things. See? I don't think it would really take too long."

"You have a beautiful body, Ann. I suppose you know that."

"Thank you. Do you like me to do this?

"Of course. You have gentle hands. They're—shall we say—uninhibited?"

"That's one way to put it."

8:37 P.M.

"Ann … maybe now …"

"Don't you like what I'm doing?"

"Very much. Only—maybe I'm younger than I thought I was."

"That's a little obvious, isn't it?"

"H-m-m-m! I guess it is!"

"Isn't there anything else you'd like me to do?"

"There might be—but I wouldn't ask it."

"I think I know."

"I've never experienced it, but I've been—well, curious."

"Why not? I don't mind. I'd like to please you."

"I act as if I'm talking with an analyst. My secret sex desires."

"You're quite a man, Mr. Jones!"

"Harry."

"Harry. Like this, Harry?"

"Yes … *like that!*"

9:12 P.M.

"I've never had anyone like you, Ann."

"Satisfied?"

"That's a silly question! Do we have time to smoke a cigarette before we get up?"

"I'd like one."

"Here, I'll light yours. One of the best times to enjoy a cigarette."

"I think so, too."

"Ann … something bothers me. I'd like to ask you some thing."

"How I ever got into this life?"

"How did you know?"

"Most men ask that."

"Well, how *did* you?"

"It's a long and possibly complicated story, Harry. I could give you a fictional explanation. I could tell you the truth, but I'd rather not. Let's just say things turned out this way."

"Don't you ever want to get out of it?"

"Sometimes. And I could. It's a way of life. That's all, Harry. Everyone has a way of life, and this is mine."

"I suppose so. Only it seems … well, you ought to have better, if you know what I mean."

"You're very nice, Harry, and I like you. I had a good time with you. I hope you had a good time with me. Maybe another time if you come to see Mr. Morrin again?"

"It's been a revealing experience, Ann. Maybe that sounds a little academic. But you've probably guessed that I haven't—well, never mind. I've enjoyed it, Ann."

"I'll have to go in a few moments. As I said, it's been fun, Harry. You're pretty terrific!"

"Well, you're not so bad yourself, young lady!"

When she was dressed and ready to leave, Harry Jones tucked a twenty-dollar bill into her pocketbook.

"Something extra—Morrin said it wasn't necessary, and I guess you have an arrangement. But I'd like you to buy yourself something you wouldn't ordinarily buy."

"I will, Harry. I honestly will. You've been nice and I appreciate it.'

He closed the door after her and she walked briskly to the elevator. She had spent more time than she usually spent with one of Mr. Morrin's customers, but it had been worth it. Twenty dollars worth it. Besides, Harry Jones had been nice in a sort of small-town way.

She smiled to herself as she thought about his reaction now that she had left. She was certain that he had never experienced some of the sexual techniques that she had revealed to him. He probably thought that he had verged upon the border of practices that were tainted with perversion, but the curiosity to experience those things had been there.

Younger men, she had discovered, were better-educated about sexual practices. The dividing lines between conservative sex, sophisticated sex, and overt perversion were more clearly defined in the minds of younger men. Most older men still held highly opinionated ideas about sexual deportment.

She remembered the fiftyish banker who had been mildly shocked and excited by her apparent "wantonness" when she had lifted her legs high during their relation. She could easily depict the banker's wife and the reserved sterility of proper undemonstrative, immobile coition that she undoubtedly practiced.

Outside the hotel she took a taxi to her apartment. She wanted a shower. It had been a profitable day already. Two dates for $170.

In the apartment building the desk clerk saw her and held up an envelope. She opened it and read the short note that had been written on the apartment house stationary available at the desk.

Ann:

A lot of years in some way, but not much in others. I got your address from your parents. From the looks of this establishment, your modeling job does right well by you. And I'd like to do right well by you with dinner tomorrow night—if you can make it.

Casey Shean

The note was almost a shock. She had told her parents that she was working as a model for advertising agencies, and she had given them her address. It had not seemed likely that anyone from her home town would be looking for her after all these years. To have Casey Shean suddenly appear was completely unexpected.

He had put a hotel name and his room number at the bottom of the letter.

Thoughtfully folding the note, she walked to the elevator. She wondered about Casey Shean and what had happened to him since that spring day, years before, when he had left for Butte. She didn't know what he did for a living, if he had married, or what he was like. But the very fact that he had been interested enough to find out where she was and to call on her now was intriguing in a strange, nostalgic way.

Certainly he did not know how she actually earned a living. She had been very careful about avoiding anyone from Montana. She actually had accepted a few modeling jobs and could fall back upon the experience; a few magazine ads in which she was pictured, and the few times she had appeared on television to substantiate a legitimate existence.

Suddenly she knew that she wanted to see and talk with Casey Shean. They were adult now. It would be interesting to go back through the years before and span the time to the present with a man who had once meant so much to her. It would be interesting to know how she would feel about it; what she would find out about herself.

In her apartment, still thinking about Shean, she dialed the answering service. There was a call. She recognized the number of a steady customer and called him.

"Hi, Ann," he said briskly. He sounded as if he were pleased with something. "I'm just leaving my office. Closed a big deal today and I feel good about it. Could I stop by for a drink and a small celebration?"

"Right away?"

"Within a half-hour. I want to be home by eleven."

"I'll have your drink ready for you!" she said.

It was getting close to ten. This would, in truth, be a quick trick and then she could call it a day and probably watch the late show on TV. Or she could join Clara later, after midnight, at one of the places where they all went after work.

She opened Shean's note and read it again. She put a call through to the hotel.

"I have a message for Mr. Shean," she explained. "But don't put a call through. Just put a note in his box that dinner at six will be fine and for him to call for me. Sign it 'Ann'."

A carefully polite voice repeated the instructions and Ann hung up and went to the kitchen to prepare a drink for the customer she expected. Then she remembered that she had better change the bed linen. She hadn't bothered after Blen had left.

She had just finished the task when the door chime sounded. Hurriedly she put the soiled linen in a hamper and went to let in her customer. Her work day was almost finished.

CHAPTER THREE

Shortly before midnight she got out of a taxi and went into a back street night club called The Beard. The building was nondescript, the street was adjacent to warehouses and loading platforms. There was nothing glamorous, expensive-looking, nor distinctive about the place except the place itself, its location, and the amusement it offered to the clientele it served.

This was the current haunt of Mike Lane and his friends of similar enterprise. Of necessity it also was the gathering place of the girls who supported them.

At one corner of the night club a small combo was busy, its music free, easy, and heavily accented, at the moment, with the jazz influence. Local artists had used the walls for large, colorful murals in *avant-garde* treatment. A small bar did a good business. At the end of the bar was an *expresso* coffee setup. This was largely for show. The bar was getting most of the business. Although the name might imply the beatnik influence, there was more of an after-hours feel to the place.

A very small part of the room was cleared for dancing, and was being used by several couples who moved their feet little, and appeared to concentrate mostly on bodily insinuations to accompnay the beat of the music.

After Ann's last customer had left (he had to be home by eleven) Clara Lindy had called her and suggested meeting at The Beard. Now Ann stood near the entrance looking for her friend.

She frowned when she saw Clara was with Mike and Cal Marker. She wondered if Marker and Mike Lane had set up the date.

Before she could change her mind about joining them, Clara saw her and waved. Ann skirted tables to where they sat. She knew that Cal Marker watched her approach with appraising eyes that missed no detail of her body, her walk, her bearing. Despite the dislike that she seemed to be deliberately engendering for the man, she caught herself subconsciously preening a little: thrusting out the allure of her breasts, subtly swaying her hips.

She was aware, too, of another man's new interest, possibly caused by Marker's obvious desire. Mike Lane was appraising her as closely as was Marker. He was a lean, blond, well-groomed man in his early thirties. He lacked the young-executive look of his friend, Marker, but he might have been mistaken for someone from the background of the theater or television—a director, or assistant producer, or possibly an agent, which in truth he was—for a certain type of talent.

As she crossed the room, she looked at the crowd and identified people she knew. She recognized a pusher who probably was supplying Mike Lane with the heroin he was using. She saw two girls who made a good living as boosters—shoplifters. At a table a young, frantic-appearing girl feverishly talked with the pusher. As Ann passed them she heard the girl's voice:

"… please, Whitey. I'm bogue. I've got to have a fix. Please. I can't cop now. But I'll have bread tomorrow. I'll pay you. I'll do anything …"

Two obvious homosexuals passed her, talking in animated, affected voices:

"… and he actually accused me of macking—actually! Me! A pimp! …"

The combo worked into a new number and two women joined the small group on the floor. They danced together intimately. No one seemed to notice them.

Two men from a local TV station were at the bar, accompanied by a thin brunette, whom Ann recognized as another call girl, and a young yellow-haired girl who occasionally appeared on TV screens. They obviously had been drinking hard and fast.

Neither of the two men at the table offered to get up when she joined them. For a second she thought of a cutting remark, but she sat down instead. This was another side of her life that she had learned to fit into effortlessly, accepting its peculiar standards of behavior, its language, its concepts with a resigned tolerance.

In some ways it was not as bad as it might have been. The after-hours people, like those in The Beard on this night, reflected a fairly large cross-section of interesting people.

She long ago had learned that there could be a strange excitement in the blend of the underworld with the more tolerant and experienced from the legitimate side of life.

If mobsters might play in The Beard, so might writers, musicians, actors, and prominent names that backgrounded the world of professional sports.

Even the language was a composite of underworld, theater, sports, and the city room of a newspaper—it seemed to be understood by all the participants of the late-hours life.

Now Mike—more friendly than usual—allowed Ann a thin smile of welcome. "Clara said you'd make the scene," he said.

Cal Marker gave her his Ivy League smile with a lift of the quizzical eyebrow. "Drink, baby?"

Ann shrugged. Suddenly it seemed pointless to make a thing of how she felt about him, even if she could logically have interpreted her feelings.

"She drinks gimlets," Clara volunteered. She directed the information toward Cal Marker, almost as if she detected Mike's sudden interest in Ann, and now hoped to divert Ann and Marker completely toward one another.

Ann suspected that the earlier quarrel between Clara and Mike had not been smoothed over. She also was sensitive to Clara's worry about Mike, and because she felt a need to reassure Clara, she forced herself to be pleasant to Marker. If Mike was interested in her, she certainly was not interested in Mike, and she wanted Clara to be certain of that fact.

"I've never seen you in here before," Ann said to Marker, making conversation.

He shrugged. "I've only been here a couple of times. Mike digs it more than I do. But tonight was different."

"Oh?"

"I wanted to see you again."

"You're wasting your time."

"No time with you is wasted."

"Why don't you give up?"

"I want to talk business." He looked away from her and watched the activity in the place. The combo was working hard. Another couple of women had joined the first couple on the floor.

Ann said, "I told you once, the answer is no."

Mike interrupted, nodding toward the door.

"Fuzz," he said.

Ann looked at the two men who had just come in. Both were middle-aged. They didn't look like detectives.

"Crowley and Bjork," Mike said. "Vice."

Ann knew them by name, but had never seen them before. She inspected them closely, making certain that she would recognize either of them again. So far she never had tangled with the police. Being able to identify fuzz, especially men from the vice squad, was important to any girl "in the life."

"They're fairly new, aren't they?" she asked Mike.

He nodded. "Old in the business, but new on the squad," he said. "They used to work bunco."

"I hate rollers," Clara said viciously. "Fuzz, rollers, nailers—cops. I hate them."

Cal looked at her with interest. "You sound as if you have reason?"

"I have. I've been busted four times. Vice cops each time. If I didn't have Mike, I don't know what would have happened to me. He got me out in a hurry." She looked significantly at Ann, "A girl needs a man sometimes," she added.

"That's what I've been telling her," Cal said lazily. "A girl never knows when she'll need a man."

"That's right, kid," Mike said, looking directly into Ann's eyes.

She shook her head. "Not interested," she said.

"Look, baby," Mike said earnestly. "Don't be an outlaw. Next thing you know you're working the street, playing around the hot-bed hotels for five bucks a trick. A girl without a man doesn't have a chance."

"Maybe I'd rather be that—a hustler—than a barnyard hen in some mack's stable," Ann said bluntly.

Cal Marker interrupted with an affected, amused drawl, "I don't think you'd be just a barnyard hen in any man's stable. You're not run-of-the-mill. You'd be head chick."

She put sarcasm into her voice: "And who's *your* head chick?"

"Maybe *you* could be."

"With how many wives-in-law, sweet daddy?"

He continued to smile at her, but she thought that the green in his eyes became a shade darker and the small muscles around his mouth tightened a trifle.

"Don't push it," he said quietly.

The cool, quiet timbre of his voice was almost like an underline to an angry command. Despite her resolution to hold him at arm's length, Cal's warning made her feel chastised and apprehensive.

Clara finished a drink and put her glass down.

"I agree with Ann," she said defiantly, her drinks talking a little for her. "I wouldn't be a barnyard hen for any man. I'd rather be an outlaw. And Mike knows how I feel about wives-in-law."

"Yeah, I know," Mike said. He wasn't smiling. He looked away from the table toward the bar and his eyes settled on a young bleached blonde who sat there alone. "There's a chick I want to see," he said. He got up and went over to the bar. He said something to the girl and she smiled. He put an arm around her as he pulled a stool closer to hers. He sat beside her and ordered.

The three at the table watched him in silence. Clara's anger was showing in her face. She took a deep breath and stood.

"I'm going home," she said.

Ann started to get up to leave with her, but Cal's hand detained her.

"Do you want me to go with you?" Ann asked Clara.

Clara shook her head, attempting to smile. It was evident that she hoped that Mike would follow her to the apartment where they lived.

"There's no use spoiling your evening," she said. She was trying hard to keep her eyes away from the bar where Mike and the girl were in intimate conversation.

Clara walked quickly to the doorway and left the club. Ann and Cal watched her. When she was gone, Ann looked at Cal Marker.

"Mike shouldn't have done that to her," she said. "She does her best for him."

Cal shrugged. "It's their problem. I've got my own. You."

"I'm not your problem. I'm nothing of yours."

"Let's cut out of here."

"It's no use. I won't buy."

He shook his head. "As a favor. Those two rollers have an eye on me. I don't like them. They don't like me. I don't want any trouble."

"Then why don't you go? I won't mind."

Suddenly he smiled, and there was something infectious about it. This was a side to Cal Marker that she had not seen before. He could be charming.

"Let's call if off for an hour or so," he said. "It's a nice night. I've got the Jag outside. We can take a ride."

She glanced toward the bar just in time to see Mike and the young blonde get up from their stools and head for the doorway. Evidently Clara was going to have a long wait.

"Bad news for Clara," Cal said bluntly, nodding toward the departing couple. "It wouldn't be, though, if she played it right. Mike's all right. He just needs bread. He's got a big bee now. He's getting to be an oil burner. It takes a lot of bread."

"So he needs a lot of horse to satisfy the monkey he carries," Ann said, reverting to the idiom of the place. "He has to do this to Clara? She's a star. You know she is. So does Mike."

"She'd still be head chick," Cal said, "So what's a wife-in-law or two when a girl's head chick? She'll just have someone else sharing the work with her."

"Don't forget she'll be sharing the man," Ann said shortly. "If it meant anything to her."

"Bitter again?" Cal asked. "Don't take it out on me. I'll make the proposition again. A simple ride out into the country. No more. No less. Buy it?"

Their eyes locked and Ann found herself nodding.

The night was warm. A full moon hung over the mountain road Cal had found with the low, fast car. Ann rested her head back and relaxed. They drove for almost an hour before he parked on a viewpoint by the highway. They looked out over the moon-drenched landscape in silence. He didn't put an arm around her, nor touch her in any way. Finally he spoke, casually and conversationally.

"Will you listen to me without flipping?" he asked. "You don't have to do anything but say 'no' if you don't like what I have to say. That's simple enough, isn't it?"

"I suppose so," she smiled. After all, he had a right to ask her, she supposed. She was in the life, and so was he, and business was business. She knew what her answer would be, but let him ask. "Ask me," she said.

"It's still no?" he asked.

"Yes, it's no."

"Okay. That's part of it. Listen to another?"

"Ask."

"Would you work a circus with one of my girls? Next week, and there's two hundred in it for you. A small, select party of business executives. They like to watch."

"No circuses."

"Maybe it isn't what you think. The other girl's a star, too. It's not as if you'd be performing with a hustler. She's in your class. Maybe you know her. Molly Easton."

Ann nodded. "I've met her. I didn't know she worked for you."

He shrugged. "She's working for me. You'd still be head chick, baby."

"No, again."

"Okay. That's the way it is."

He lit cigarettes for them and they smoked them in silence, enjoying the night. When they had finished the cigarettes and put them out, he started the car and turned back toward the city. Ann liked the surge and speed of the Jaguar, and had to admit to herself that the man went with the car. He looked smart and smooth and sophisticated behind the wheel. He looked like anything but what he was. She wondered about his past, and how he happened to get into the business that supported him.

On the point of asking him, she changed her mind. It was none of her business and she didn't want him to think that she was interested in him.

He drove fast and well. It was almost two o'clock when he parked in front of the apartment where she lived. The street was almost deserted of traffic. He turned off the car lights.

"Buy me a nightcap?" he smiled.

She hesitated about taking him up to her apartment, and then wondered why she did. After all, she wasn't an innocent virgin. Nor was he a high school boy or a misunderstood husband on the make. As a matter of fact, he had a stable of girls to satisfy his needs, and undoubtedly would leave her to go to one of them now. She wondered if he rotated himself among them. She knew that some pimps did, while others made it a rule to stay with the girl who had brought in the most money for a night.

At any rate, she didn't have to worry about any of that, and he *had* taken her for an enjoyable drive, he had *not* made himself objectionable during the drive, and she certainly could afford a friendly drink to round off the evening. She seldom went to bed before three or four, anyhow, and doubted if he did better. It was all part of the life.

"Come up," she smiled.

In the apartment she put on a record, with the amplifier turned low, and went to the kitchen to mix drinks. He went with her.

"You're sure about the circus?" he asked.

"Positive." Although sex was a commercial thing to her, she had never liked the thought of putting on an exhibition with another woman to whet the appetites of the men who watched.

He shrugged again and accepted the drink she had mixed. They went into the living room. He stopped and listened to the music, nodding approval. He took her glass and put it on a table beside his. Without asking her, he drew her lightly in his arms and they danced.

For the first time in many months she was dancing with a man who was not buying her. Almost reluctantly her hand crept around the back of his neck and she came a little closer to him, very much aware of the hard, masculine flatness of his body. He moved easily and surely, almost with tiger grace.

"Well! What do you know!" he grinned. "We're dancing."

"You do it well," she conceded.

"And you." He pulled her closer and they moved in silence until the record ended. He didn't let her go, but still held her, looking down into her face.

"Let's forget business," he said.

"There isn't any to forget," she said. She wondered if he was going to kiss her, and if she would turn her lips away.

She didn't. His lips were hard and demanding. Her mouth opened to his and she felt his hands. It seemed futile to try to stop him. She shut her eyes and let the moment take care of itself. She could handle him with a cold lack of response at the right time. So let him try ...

When he lifted her and carried her toward the bedroom she opened her eyes. For a second she thought of demanding to be let down, but the small and charming smile was on his lips and in his eyes again.

"Do you mind?" he asked.

"Should I?" she said. "It won't mean anything. Why bother?"

"Let's find out."

He put her down gently on the bed and undressed her with certain, experienced fingers. She let him have his way, surprised at her acquiescence, yet strangely pleased with his attention, and frankly inquisitive about what he would do.

She was so accustomed to taking the initiative and providing the skilled techniques of love making in a professional capacity, that there was a feeling of pleasure and odd relief in shutting her eyes and surrendering herself to the skilled ministrations of this man who regarded love making as professionally as she did.

Then—sometime during the next hour, the exact moment or gesture or movement of which she never was certain—a new relationship between them was born in intensity of emotions and sensations such as she never had experienced before.

The hour had started with her deliberate surrender to relaxation and enjoyment; with his skilled attentions and innovations that were successful in arousing her out of professional lethargy with an acceptance of compatablility for both of them.

It had started with kisses and caresses and explorations. It had continued with certainty and accomplishment. It had reached a logical and pleasant moment of union by calm moments of resting and waiting before the intricacies of rhythms were begun.

And somewhere along this familiar journey that she had experienced so many, many times, the landmarks were lost and the highway soared up and beyond the experienced.

Was it the moment when his hands pinioned her arms above her head in a gesture of conquest? Was it the moment when his lips were alive at her mouth and forced her to give freely? Was it the moment when his voice was low and certain and he said, "You're mine."?

Or was it the sweetly exquisite moment when very briefly she was back through the years with Casey Shean on the night before he left for Butte—a memory that was only seconds brief in the moment, yet poignant enough to break the last barrier?

Oddly the first words she cried, as the exquisite ecstasy began, were: "Casey ... oh, Casey." Then it was beyond Casey and a memory of a night long ago; beyond all the experiences and nights and men she had known in the full sense of being a woman.

She moaned and her mouth opened in the expression of a scream, but no scream came from her lips. She grasped desperately at Cal Marker, and blindly sought to draw closer to him; hopelessly grateful when he understood her need and held her with straining arms and hands as he brought her to a summit she never had achieved before—not with Casey, nor with any other man nor in any other way. When it was finished she was completely limp and weak beyond the strength to lift a hand or open her eyes.

Afterward, they lay apart from one another, breathing deeply and in a strange exhaustion. Below them, in the street, tires shrieked as a car sped around a corner. In the apartment kitchen the electric icebox clicked and began to sound as if a motor was running quietly in the night.

I won't think about it, Ann thought. I won't think about it yet. I can't.

After a while she left the bed and walked to the bathroom. When she returned to the bedroom she went to a closet and found a robe. She put it on and lit a cigarette.

Cal Marker had not dressed, but lay idly smoking on the bed, a pillow bunched under his head, watching her with a sardonic look of amusement.

"Good?" he asked.

She returned his look, seeking a defense against this man who had brought her an experience she never before had know so completely, even with Casey.

"You know how it was," she said flatly. "Now, why don't you dress and get out of here?"

"I could stay," he suggested.

"And disappoint whichever one of your stable is waiting for you? Don't do it. Keep your girls happy. I don't need you."

"I think you do."

"Will you please get out of here?"

They smoked in silence, their eyes locked. He finished his cigarette and carefully extinguished it in an ash tray on a bedside table. He got up slowly and easily so that his finely muscled body was displayed in a masculine, catlike grace. She tried not to watch him, but couldn't take her eyes away from his movements.

She watched him dress—not awkwardly, but quickly and neatly. He knotted his tie with casual ease, and slipped into his suit jacket. When he was ready to leave, he led the way to the hallway door and looked at her as she waited defiantly for him to open the door and go out.

"Good night, baby," he smiled. Smoothly he reached cut and grasped one of her arms and pulled her close. Before she could break away, he had cupped her chin with his free hand and was kissing her.

He released her as suddenly as he had claimed her. She wiped her mouth with the back of a hand and glared at him.

"You son-of-a-bitch," she said softly. "You dirty, pimp son-of-a-bitch."

The green eyes narrowed. Hardly seeming to move, his right hand flashed out and slapped her sharply across the face. She fell back with the shock of the blow, her eyes opening wide.

"Don't ever call me that again," he said softly. "My women don't call me that." He watched her back away another step, his green eyes austerely cold and dispassionate.

Then he spoke again, in the same soft voice: "And you're my woman now. Don't you ever forget it."

He turned and left the apartment, closing the door quietly behind him. For a moment Ann stared at the closed door, trying to realize what had happened.

In a wave of frustrated rage she picked up a fragile ceramic ash tray from the coffee table near her knees. She threw the tray at the closed door. It crashed and pieces fell to the floor.

Ann looked at the mark she had made on the door and at the remains of the shattered tray on the floor. His words were echoing and re-echoing through her mind: *And you're my woman now.* The moments in the bedroom were a part of her. What he had done to her, and what he had brought her, were things that would always be a part of her now and could never be undone nor forgotten. Suddenly she was sick with the realization.

CHAPTER FOUR

She had a Tuesday morning dental appointment at eleven o'clock. The dentist was a soft-spoken, gray-haired man with a very professional attitude. He called her "Miss Freeman" and was very careful not to allow even the front of his white jacket to brush against her shoulder as he worked.

"Your teeth are in excellent conditon," he told her. "They hardly need cleaning."

She smiled at him with her eyes, wondering why he usually became conversational when his patient had a wide-open mouth.

"It's a pleasure to have a patient who takes such good care of her teeth," he said.

She smiled with her eyes again and patiently submitted to his teeth-cleaning operations.

She recognized, almost subconsciously, that she had a slight obsession about cleanliness. She realized that she took more baths than most women ordinarily took, but it seemed to be part of business for her. Not only did she want to be clean and fresh for her customers, but afterwards she wanted to be cleansed of her relations with the customers.

Health and hygiene were important to a girl "in the life." A venereal disease could mean disaster, even if the cures were almost routine in these days of miracle drugs. Some girls she knew insisted upon having preventive antibiotic shots periodically to ward off the possibility of contracting a disease.

"Feminine hygiene" was frequently discussed among her acquaintances in the business. Ann always thought of the phrase in two concepts: one, as a concept of cleanliness in relation to her body, especially those parts concerned with sex; the second, involved the problem of contraception.

Sally Smith, the first prostitute she ever had known, and the girl who had introduced her into the business, had talked about that particular problem.

"You should make up your mind what you want to do about it," Sally had explained three years before when Ann had decided to go into "the life." "Whichever way you go, you'll have to realize that you can hardly ever expect a man to take care of that part of it. Men expect you to take the responsibility."

"What do *you* do, Sally?" Ann had asked.

"I use a diaphragm. Most girls—who *do* use anything— do that."

"You mean some girls don't use anything at all?"

"Some have a theory that when you're with a lot of different men you don't get pregnant. I think that perhaps they're just lucky."

"But some girls don't?"

"That's right. And, as a matter of fact, back in the old days I guess the girls working in the big houses never used anything, either."

Sally thoughtfully had mixed another light drink for them on this particular evening spent in Sally's apartment, and she had continued with the instructive conversation.

"A girl in the racket has a lot of unusual little problems like that," she had explained. "Abortions. You've got to set aside some money to take care of those. And you ought to have regular physical checkups."

Thoughtfully she had held up her drink and looked at it. "This too. You'd better not drink too much. Men don't like girls who don't hold their drinks and get sloppy—not the girls they are buying. If they're on the make for a square—some gal they've got to seduce—then they like to get 'em tight."

In the dentist's chair, Ann shut her eyes while the doctor meticulously continued with his task. She had not thought about Sally Smith for a long time, and she didn't know what had become of her. Sally had gone to New York with her man. There had been a few scribbled letters and then nothing more.

Thinking about Sally now, Ann remembered the first time she herself had taken money from a man for her bedroom services.

After she had left Missoula, there had been jobs in a few offices, then some modeling work, some TV assignments doing commercials, and then somehow she had fallen into a pattern of parties and men and waking up too often in strange bedrooms.

One night at a party for some visiting businessmen she met Sally Smith. They had liked one another at once and in the days that followed a friendship was established. Ann knew what Sally did for a living, and there was no pretense about it.

At the time Ann was out of work, and she was confiding her problems to Sally on a winter afternoon.

"I have to get some money somewhere," she said.

"I can let you have some," Sally told her.

"Thanks, hon, but that wouldn't solve anything. I have to earn some money, and I simply haven't been able to find a decent job. Modeling is slow and I'm not quite good enough for the better jobs. It's the same with TV. And I despise office work."

"Well," Sally said thoughtfully, "you could do what I'm doing."

Ann felt that she should be deeply shocked by the suggestion, but she was not. She gazed thoughtfully at Sally's finely molded face—that later she would see bruised and broken by Sally's man—and she remembered the times she had gone to bed with men. There had been a good many since Casey, and none of them had been anything but an unsatisfactory experience. Sometimes she wondered if a deep quest to find satisfaction was the driving force that sent her from bed to bed.

Whatever might have been the motivation, the fact was real and concrete. She certainly had not been living a chaste life, nor did she particularly consider herself to be in search of marriage.

Oddly, at that moment with Sally, she remembered the last night with Casey and her insistence that he call her a whore. There had been something in it that night, and she had responded to it. Maybe some women were intended to be whores. Maybe that was why they were born.

"I've never taken money for it," she told Sally.

"Why not? You didn't always do it for love, did you? Or just for kicks. Or *was* it for kicks?"

"No. It doesn't mean much to me. I did it because—well, it was easier to do it than not to do it. Can you understand that?"

"Certainly. What girl in the life couldn't?" Sally smiled.

"If I did want to—how would I get started?"

"There's a deal next Saturday night. It's a convention job. I can line you up. It'll be fifty dollars a trick, and you could take care of several during the night. Not too many of us are working it, and there are a couple of dozen men."

Ann thought about the date she had for that Saturday night. It was with a man who was almost a casual friend, yet with whom she had gone to bed a half dozen times. Actually she had little more than an indifferent liking for him. He was just one of a good many.

"How much do you think I'd make?" she asked.

"Possibly two hundred or two-fifty. Maybe even more."

"I've never—I mean, I've only been with one man in an evening, except on a couple of parties that ran wild. I don't know if I could take it, Sally."

"Don't worry. They'll be quick tricks. Most of them are if you want them to be. You're smart enough to know what makes them quick."

Sally's frankness made Ann smile. "I could use a couple of hundred, and I don't suppose it would be any worse than going to bed with the date I have for that night."

"Certainly not. Break your date and I'll line this up for you."

"If I got started, how would I get more business?"

"I'll help you. I've more names in my black book than I can handle. I'll give you some of the names. Only don't let *him* know."

"All right. I'll break my date."

The Saturday night job had not been as bad as she had anticipated. The men were salesmen and they had been drinking, but they held their liquor well. Several rooms in the hotel had been placed at the disposal of the girls, and they entertained in them, returning to the large banquet room where the main party was in progress.

The first man she had taken to one of the rooms was a shy young salesman from Ohio. He had treated her as he might have treated a date from his home town. The performance on the bed was short and energetic. He thanked her afterwards and with an embarrassed grin he put a ten-dollar bill on the dresser top.

"I guess you—I mean, it's paid for," he stumbled. "That's what they told me. But I don't want—I mean, I'd like to add this."

She smiled. "Thanks. It was fun. I mean it. Really fun."

He left the room obviously pleased by her remark. Ann took the money and the calling card he had given her. Her payment from the firm would be made upon presentation of the various calling cards of the men she served to the sales manager who was managing the sales convention.

As she dressed and got ready to return to the banquet room, she tried to decide how she felt about herself; what difference this had made to her; if she felt debased, or low, or vastly different.

The physical experience, as usual, had meant virtually nothing. The young man had been pleasant and she had enjoyed a brief satisfaction in making him happy. She already had been too promiscuous to be bothered much about the intimacy with a stranger, and she admitted this to herself.

She returned to the party and before the night was over she had come back to the bedroom five times. The following week Sally gave her names from the black book and within a few weeks Ann Freeman was firmly intrenched in "the life…."

"There, Miss Freeman. That should do you for another six months."

The dentist's voice brought her out of her reverie and she took the glass of water he handed her and rinsed. Her mouth felt clean and fresh, and her gums were just a trifle tender from the cleaning.

She thanked the dentist and in the outer waiting room she paid her bill and made an appointment for her return in six months.

The girl attendant was friendly and openly envious of the clothing Ann wore.

"That's an awfully attractive frock, Miss Freeman. Did you buy it here in the city? It looks like New York."

"No, I got it here," Ann smiled. She didn't go on to explain that she had bought it from a very nervous old man who operated from a single office room in an old building. The clothing he sold was brought to him by the boosters who worked the stores in the city. He sold the garments for a fraction of their retail value. Virtually every call girl whom Ann knew traded with him.

She left the medical building and had a cup of coffee at a drugstore lunch counter. Her thoughts in the dentist's chair—remembering how she had started in "the life"—seemed to have a significance for her because of what had happened the night before.

Since the first night when she had accepted money, she had worked alone. She had built her clientele list in her little black book, and Sally had left her additional names when she left for New York. Never had there been a man involved in the background to accept the money she earned, to take her earnings and give her a semblance of protection and attention in return.

Nor had any man ever brought to her the fulfillment she had experienced the night before. Now, as she drank her coffee, she let herself think deliberately about Cal Marker, and face the fact that she might be in trouble with him. This was no man to be dismissed lightly. He had left his mark upon her as certainly as if he had scarred her physically.

She knew as certainly as she knew what had happened to her that she would be irresistibly drawn to him, even as she might hate him. That she would despise him, yet want him with equal intensity. The frightening fact was that she couldn't understand why she felt as she did about him; and that now—for the first time—she could truly understand how Clara might feel about Mike.

But there might be a certain escape from what Cal Marker might have started the night before. Tonight she would meet

Casey Shean. Some people said that you couldn't go back. She usually was inclined to agree with them. Certainly she could never go back to what she once had been simply because you couldn't turn back the years. You could not recapture girlish innocence. You could not erase the men and places and trauma of the years. But perhaps you could recapture a basic emotion, a deep feeling for someone else.

"It probably won't mean a thing," she told herself. "He'll be changed. I'll probably be bored." Despite her realistic self-assurances, she subconsciously hoped that she would be wrong.

In the drugstore she checked with her answering service. There were no calls. She shopped for an hour and had a quick light lunch in the tearoom of a department store. It was two o'clock in the afternoon when she returned to the apartment building.

The elevator door opened and Mike Lane stepped out. He lived with Clara in the apartment a couple of floors above Ann's but it was seldom that he and Ann met in the building. Today he seemed to be pleased to find her waiting.

He stepped back into the elevator. "I'll go up with you, Ann," he smiled. "I want to talk with you."

The elevator operator looked at Lane with a concealed glance of distaste and then glanced at Ann. She smiled at the old man. To Mike Lane she said, "I'm in a hurry, Mike. Perhaps we'd better postpone it."

"I'll only take a moment," Mike assured her. He nodded at the elevator operator. Ann shrugged slightly. The operator closed the door and the elevator went up.

Mike followed her to the apartment door and inside the apartment. He closed the door after him and without waiting for an invitation he sat in an easy chair and lit a cigarette.

"Well?" Ann asked him.

"Look, baby—Cal's a nice guy, but he's not for you."

"That's not news. Is that all—"

He held up a cautioning hand and smiled. "Hold it. Wait until I finish, baby. It's just that if you're as smart as I think you are, you'll be shopping for a man. When you need him, I want you to know that I'll take care of you better than Cal—or anyone. You ought to know that. You know bow I look after Clara."

"And why will I need a man?"

"Did you see those two rollers look you over last night?"

"I didn't notice."

"Well, they did. But good. They've got you tabbed. And I'd hate to have anyone tip them where, who, and how you're doing business."

"Meaning someone like you?"

"Meaning they could catch up with you. You could fall. A couple of nailers like those two would like to bring in a star like you. And when they do—who's going to go down and put up bail? Who's going to take care of your protection?"

"I'll handle it if the time comes."

"How? You don't think you could George either of those two and buy your way out of a fall, do you? Not Crowley nor Bjork. Even if you could get 'em interested enough to lay you, they wouldn't leave you. They'd take you in."

"Get to the point, Mike. What do you want?"

"What do *you* think?"

"Either yarding or macking," she said acidly. "I'm having neither. If you want to sleep with someone behind Clara's back, it won't be me. She's my friend. As for the other—I've already turned down one offer, and you appeal to me even less than Cal does."

Mike smashed out his cigarette. "You'll change your mind," he said.

He got up and walked toward her door. She noticed that he was much thinner than when she first knew him. He had developed several nervous mannerisms. His dope habit was beginning to show.

She realized, too, that undoubtedly he had changed in other ways. Now that he was hooked by the habit, he would be relentless in his efforts to get money to support it. There could be danger in his veiled threats of what might happen to her if she didn't join Clara under his protection and to his advantage.

"Wait a second," she said as he reached for the doorknob. "Let's get something straight. I don't want any trouble. Don't give me any, Mike. Don't try to involve me with you and Clara. Just leave me alone."

"Sure, baby, sure! Don't worry about me. Just worry about the fuzz like Crowley and Bjork. And remember when you need help that you'll be better off with a guy like me than a guy like Cal Marker who's worrying about four other girls. You'll always know where you stand with me."

He opened the door and went out, his departing smile laden with unspoken significance. She didn't believe that he would ever set her up for the cops—he had the reputation for being regular—but when a man needed money for a big habit he might do anything to get a girl working for him. The demands of morphine reach far.

She checked with the answering service again. A Mr. Calman wanted her to call. She recognized another job for a business firm. Calman had the title of sales promotion manager for a local firm that sold nationally. He probably had an important customer in the city.

She made the call and Calman asked her if she would be available. She remembered her date with Casey Shean, and she remembered that she had earned extra money the day before. She could afford a lighter day now.

"I probably won't be free until late in the evening," she said.

"How late?"

"Probably eleven o'clock."

"That'll be okay. We're having a business conference until around nine tonight and there'll be a few drinks afterwards. But he specifically wants someone. He asked me about it."

"Is this an all-night date?"

"I don't think so. But he's important to us. We'd appreciate some good co-operation, if you get what I mean. As a matter of fact, there could be double the usual if you please him."

"Eleven o'clock," Ann said. She got the man's name and his hotel suite number. Now she could well afford to take off the first part of the evening with Casey. After all, she had only a dinner date. She was assuming that there would be nothing more than a couple of hours at dinner with conversation. She might well be free by nine o'clock, but she decided to keep free until the eleven o'clock date.

With luck she might get a hair-do this afternoon. She wanted especially to look good for Casey Shean; like the model he thought she was.

She called Marcel's beauty salon and was lucky to get a date at three o'clock. She dialed her answering service and cut off calls to her, and then, after a brief hesitation, she dialed Clara's number. Clara answered at once.

They made small talk for a few moments, and then Ann casually asked if the quarrel with Mike had been patched up.

"Right after I left," Clara said. "He almost beat me home."

Ann knew that she was lying, but she knew that Clara would never admit that Mike probably had spent the night with the blonde from the bar. She also knew that Clara had deep fits of depression and she had been worried. On one occasion Clara had swallowed a half bottle of sleeping pills— fortunately during a quarrel with Mike and while he was there to take care of her.

But never before had Ann known Mike to actively seek another woman to work for him, and she was apprehensive about what it could do to Clara.

"I guess I was just worried about you," she said.

Clara forced a small laugh. "What's to worry, hon? I'm all right. It's this boy kick he's on."

"Boy?"

"Boy for morphine. Girl for cocaine."

"Oh. I guess I knew that. I wonder why girl for cocaine."

"They say they get a sex kick out of the stuff. Like girl."

"I'm glad I've never played with any of it," Ann said.

"Not even joy-pop?"

"No. Not even pot."

"I've smoked the weed. But I guess I'm like you. I want my kicks, but not that way."

"I'd better cut this short," Ann said, glancing at her watch. "I'm going to have my hair done and I've a dinner date with an old friend."

"You mean like a square setting?"

"That's right. Like a square setting. It's a guy I knew back home. He doesn't know what I do, so I'm not working."

"Have fun," Clara said. Her voice sounded a little more cheerful. "Will you make the scene later?"

"Probably. I've a date with a John at eleven."

"Later then."

They hung up and Ann took a lazy tub bath and then dressed in a casual skirt and blouse. She could dress for dinner after she returned from the beauty salon.

Before she left, and purely from impulse, she dug into the bottom of a dresser drawer and got out a savings deposit book and checked her total savings. This was her emergency fund; her security. This was the fund the attorney could draw upon if necessary.

Looking at it and seeing the $3,000 total gave her a measure of reassurance after Mike's visit and veiled warnings about the two members of the vice squad.

"I'd be crazy to team with a man," she told herself. "He'd have this money and everything else, too. And I'd have nothing but a man to keep. I'll pay it my way. Not Mike's!"

Although she named Mike, she knew that she really meant Cal Marker, and even as she put away the bankbook she found herself thinking about the Jag and the money it must take to keep Cal Marker in the style he obviously liked. She wondered how many other girls had been able to give Cal Marker $3,000 in a lump sum!

Well, now that she faced it, neither Mike nor Cal Marker would ever see any of that money, nor any other money that she earned. She didn't need a status symbol. All she needed was more money in her savings accounts. Then some day maybe she could buy a smart gown shop, or open a small business of her own.

No, she didn't need Mike, nor Cal Marker, nor any man. She knew all there was to know about men, and had experienced all that they had to give her, and even what had happened between Cal Marker and her—and she hardly dared think of it—was no real proof of need.

Maybe some day in the future she might marry. There was such a thing as companionship, and even such a thing as kids. Sometimes she wished that she might have children.

And if she were ever to live that kind of life, there would have to be a man. A decent, respectable, hard-working man who would probably be faithful to her, and whom she could love skillfully and well so that he never would be interested in another woman; a man, perhaps, like Casey Shean.

She went to the door wondering if he had changed much; if he would look something out of the backwoods; if he would be too flashily dressed, too confident, too uninteresting.

During the last fifteen minutes or so, after she had finished dressing and was waiting for him, she realized that she had difficulty in picturing him in detail from memory.

She could remember his tall height, his Irish cast of features, the unruly hair, the breadth of shoulders. But the minute details of feature, the exactness of voice, the texture of skin, touch of hands, habits of gesture were all more or less lost with the years.

Too, there had been the other questions. Was he married? What did he do for a living? What was he doing in this city? How long would he be here? Was she wise in seeing him even this once?

She made a last small inspection of herself in a mirror near the doorway, and then she opened the door and he was standing there.

Neither spoke in that first appraising look that had to span the years. She knew what he saw, and she was certain of herself and her appearance. Her whole curiosity was in the man before her.

He had matured. The Irish face had taken on a fine edge of maturity and strength. The eyes were steady and friendly. The broad shoulders were a little heavier, but he was trim of waist and flat of stomach. He was tanned a deep brown and he was hatless. A very small edging of gray—almost premature, considering that he was still in his early thirties—touched his temples.

He was well tailored, well groomed, and he looked prosperous. He smiled and his teeth were almost startling white against his tan.

"Ann!" he exclaimed. "No wonder you model! You're lovely."

"Irish!" she laughed. "Come in Casey. Come in and let me really look at you."

Then, before he crossed the threshold, and before she could stop him, he had placed his strong, lean hands on her shoulders, held her, and kissed her hard and certainly, full on the lips.

"For old times," he said, releasing her. "And mighty good, too."

She shook her head in mock despair and led him into the apartment. The kiss had been too impulsive and unexpected to be anything but a quick, hard kiss between a man and a woman, but she had liked it, and the assertive way he had done it.

"Drink?" she asked over her shoulder.

"Just a short one. Bourbon and water, if you have it."

He followed her into the kitchen. She remembered that Cal Marker had followed her into the kitchen like this, and it disturbed her. She didn't want to think about Cal Marker. She quickly made the drinks and they returned to the living room. He sat across the room, looking at her over his glass, smiling and obviously pleased.

"Ann, you've become a really beautiful woman."

"Not beautiful, Casey. Passable. And you haven't fared too poorly yourself. I can't decide whether you look like a millionaire executive just back from the Riviera, or a hardworking engineer just off the mountain."

He laughed. "Neither. I own most of a small electronics manufacturing plant near Butte."

"Electronics? Near Butte?" she asked. "I thought most of them in the West are near Los Angeles or San Francisco."

"Why not Butte?" he asked. "We're not large and a lot of our stuff is government contract. Our location is no problem. We're happy—and prosperous."

"That's wonderful, Casey. I'm glad to hear it." Ann took a long swallow of her drink and looked at his left hand. He wore no wedding band.

"Are you married, Casey?"

"Not now. It didn't take. We were divorced three years ago. A Butte girl. You wouldn't know her."

"Children?"

"No."

"I'm sorry, Casey. About the divorce, I mean."

"Don't be. We despised each other after the first year. It was a happy ending."

For a few moments the conversation drifted around to mutual friends they had known in Montana, a reference to her folks—whom he had seen the month before—and to the changes in Missoula and Butte.

"That's enough of what was and what's changed," he finally said. "Let's talk about you, Ann. Tell me about yourself. Your folks told me that you do some modeling and that you've been on TV."

"I'm afraid it isn't very glamorous," Ann said. "I model occasionally, mostly for advertising agencies, and my TV work consists only of commercials. I had small parts in one or two productions. And, of course the stores use models. All in all, I manage to live."

He listened with interest, nodding as she spoke, as if he were eager to learn all that he could about her, and to approve of everything she did.

"You look wonderful," he said. "I mean it. And you've never married?"

She shook her head and sipped her drink. "Too busy with a career," she said. She hoped fervently that he would never learn what kind of a career she meant. "But let's save some of this. I'm starved!"

"I don't know many places around here. I'm staying at The Chateau. The dining room there is good. All right?"

"Fine," she said. The dining room there *was* good, and expensive. The cocktail lounge by the dining room was equally good and not averse to allowing some of the better girls to tarry on occasion. This was very strictly grounds for $50 girls, or more expensive ones. She only hoped that one of her customers wouldn't be there, with too many drinks under his belt.

"The etiquette of prostitution is very specific," she once had explained to Carl Blen in one of their friendly talks as they talked in bed after making love. "A girl never recognizes a customer in public unless the customer speaks to her, and even then she usually is most discreet."

"Do the customers often speak when you meet that way?"

"Seldom. If they're alone, they may. And if they've had too much to drink they can even become obnoxious. Drink does strange things to inhibitions and social behavior, Carl."

So she hoped that none of her customers would be in the place tonight, and that any who might be there would have good control of inhibitions and social behavior.

In the street Casey helped her into a taxi. At the hotel dining room a table had been reserved for them near the archway that opened upon the more dimly lighted cocktail lounge.

The atmosphere of the place accented luxury. The clientele had that moneyed look about them. The fact that Casey was staying there indicated that economically he was doing well.

As he ordered cocktails and dinner, she glanced around the large room. She recognized no one and allowed herself a small sigh of relief.

Then she looked into the cocktail lounge and saw a girl she had met a few weeks before at a party. The girl was new in the business, but she had the looks and poise she needed to rate the high fees, and she looked enough like a young debutante, or a smart business girl, to sit alone at the Chateau lounge bar without causing suspicion.

Even as Ann noticed her, the girl glanced at Ann and there was a slight, friendly smile of recognition before she looked away and directed her attention to the drink before her.

Across the table Casey lit a cigarette and toyed with the cocktail that had just been placed before him. He seemed to be deliberately studying her, as if he might be trying to evaluate her, to answer an unspoken question in his mind.

"Something wrong?" Ann asked.

"Wrong?"

"The way you're looking at me."

"Oh. That." He picked up his drink and sampled it. "I was just looking at you and remembering."

"So?"

"I didn't know how lucky I was."

"That was a long time ago. Two different persons."

"I suppose so. Tell me—hasn't there been anyone, Ann? Why haven't you married? What about you?"

"No one I liked well enough," she said thoughtfully, thinking of the many, many who had liked *her* well enough. "What was your wife like, Casey? What went wrong?"

"She was too rich and too pretty and she had a weakness for adultery."

"And that you couldn't take," Ann said.

"And that I couldn't take," he nodded. "Maybe one or two I could possibly have forgiven—under certain circumstances. Five or six—that I knew about—was little better than promiscuousness in my book. She might as well have been a whore."

She might as well have been a whore. Casey—that's what I am. I'm a whore. And I'm not so sure that you didn't start me toward being one.

"There couldn't be whores without men," she said lightly, picking up her cocktail and drinking a little of it. "And at least they're more honest than the strictly promiscuous gals. They don't make any pretenses about multiple bed partners."

"Mighty frank talk," he grinned. "At least I know that you're neither."

"How can you be sure?" she smiled.

"Because I know you, Ann. Maybe it was a long time ago, and maybe we were kids and didn't know what the score was, but we were old enough to be a man and a woman. I knew what you were. I've always known."

"Do you think there have been no others, Casey?"

He put out his cigarette and lit another. "How does a man answer that question to a lovely woman?" he said, his lips in an abashed smile. "Frankly, I suppose there have. You must have had affairs of one kind or another. But I'm an understanding citizen of a modem world in which business and career girls take on a few rights of their own. So you may have. I don't want to know. It isn't important. After all, I know how it was between *us*."

"You and your Irish tongue do dodge a tough question!" she laughed.

If you knew, Casey. What would you really think? What would you say? That isn't important? Not important that I've laid several hundred men—at least that many, and probably more? I've never

counted them. I don't want to count them. 1 don't want to count
my whoring hours. Just the money. The bank accounts.

A waiter began to serve their dinner. They ate leisurely and
the conversation became filled again with the recounting of news
from Montana, the lives their friends in the university had made
for themselves, the marriages, births, deaths, successes, failures.

Then, over after-dinner coffee, she happened to glance into
the lounge and felt a small knot of fear tighten deep within her.
The girl she had greeted silently with the exchange of glances and
knowing smiles was animatedly talking with a large man who
had taken the stool beside her. The girl was smiling and display-
ing the poise and youthful beauty that made her seem anything
but what she actually was.

Perhaps it was her inexperience that was contributing to the
danger she now was in. Ann wished that someone had warned
her about cocktail lounge pickups unless a girl was certain about
the men to avoid; the situations to escape.

The man with the girl was Crowley of the vice squad.
Obviously the girl had no idea who he was and she was making
a subtle but definite play for him. Crowley was doing his job
well, ordering drinks, flashing a carefree smile—the man on
the loose for the night, looking for a good time, ready to buy an
expensive girl.

"Isn't that right, Ann?" Casey said.

She looked at him, startled. "Casey—I'm sorry, I didn't hear
what you were saying."

He nodded toward the bar. "Someone over there you know?"

"I thought I saw someone, but I guess I was mistaken. I'm
sorry, Casey. Isn't *what* right?"

He shook his head and laughed. "Just making small talk. I've
forgotten. As a matter of fact, I was really thinking that I could

probably rent a car and we could take a drive. I'd like to do that—if you would."

She glanced surreptitiously at her watch. It was a little after eight. She still had almost three hours before her date with the customer, and she didn't want to take Casey back to her apartment.

"It sounds like fun, Casey. Why don't you go out to the desk and see about arranging for the car?"

"Good. Will you wait here?"

She nodded. He got up and left her, walking with his easy stride. Several women glanced at him as he went by.

Ann looked back into the lounge. The flirtation between the girl and Crowley was progressing. They were sitting closer together, and Crowley had just ordered another drink for them. Ann looked down the length of the lounge for Crowley's partner, Bjork, but the other man was not in sight.

Crowley was drinking his drink hurriedly and apparently urging the girl to finish hers. He nodded toward the doorway. The girl was gathering together her cigarettes, lighter, and purse. Ann saw her glance toward the powder room door and say something. Ann had expected this and had been waiting for it.

As the girl went toward the door, Ann got up and followed her. When she passed behind Crowley she glanced into the back bar mirror and their eyes met. She saw a flicker of recognition in his glance and knew that he identified her from her association with Cal Marker on the previous night.

Ann found the girl in the powder room and took her to a deserted corner. "Look, hon," she said quietly, "that guy you're with is fuzz. He's Crowley from the vice squad."

The girl paled. "Oh, God! Are you sure?"

"Certain."

"I was just going to take him to my apartment. I'd even told him how much it would cost. Ann, what am I going to do?"

"You could walk out and leave him. Only he'd probably follow you. There's no back way out of here."

The girl was regaining her composure a little. She got out a lipstick and carefully applied it.

"Ann, what if I simply go over and laugh and say he's made a mistake? That I was only kidding him. And then walk out."

"He'd probably be sore, and you'd make an enemy—but he's one anyhow. You've already admitted you're in the racket. But he needs evidence to take you in."

"So at least I can deny I was hustling him."

"It's up to you."

The girl nodded and went out. Ann waited and followed a few moments later. The girl was walking away from Crowley toward the doorway. She smiled knowingly at Ann as they passed.

Ann kept her eyes straight ahead. There was a lull at the bar and Crowley was sitting alone at the end nearest the dining room. He saw Ann approach and got up from his stool and blocked her way unobstrusively, as if he were a friend greeting another.

"Hello, Ann," he smiled. "Ann Freeman. Right?"

"I'm sorry. I don't know you." She tried to get by him, but he feigned a friendly laugh and his hand clamped on her arm and pulled her close in a tight maneuver that could hardly be noticed.

"You know me, all right. That pimp Marker tipped you last night. And you just tipped the girl I had here."

"I don't know what you're talking about."

"I'm taking about that little bitch, and you, and all the rest of you girls who are peddling your ass around here. You didn't help yourself any by breaking that up tonight. I won't forget. Sooner or later I'm going to nail you. But good."

"Let me go. I still don't know what you're talking about."

"Any dame who's with Cal Marker knows what I'm talking about."

She tried to pull her arm free, but he gripped it harder.

"What's the big hurry, baby? And who's that John with you? I haven't seen him around before. Is he that? A John? Or one of Marker's pals?"

"Take your hands off me, you louse."

She pulled against his grasp and they stumbled slightly in the energy of her strength.

Suddenly another strong masculine hand was supporting her and a low, intense voice was saying. "Do you know this guy, Ann? Is he bothering you?"

Ann looked up at Casey with sudden fear. She didn't want him involved in this.

"It's all right, Casey. Let's get out of here."

"I didn't like what I saw, Ann. This lug should—"

"Take it easy, sonny," Crowley interrupted, his lips curling suggestively. "With a dame like this—"

Casey's fist connected solidly. Crowley went down. A woman at the bar screamed. The bartender hurried around the end of the bar: "Look here, mister, Take it easy, will you?" He stooped over the dazed Crowley.

"Oh, God," Ann whispered. "Please get us out of here." She pulled at Casey's arm.

He grinned down at her. "Maybe we'd better go," he said. "I've a car waiting." He hurried her out of the gathering crowd and across the lobby and into the street. No one tried to stop them. He had rented a convertible and the top was down. They slid smoothly away from the curb and into the early evening traffic.

"You didn't know him, did you?" Casey suddenly asked, anxiously. "I just saw him pull at you and I could see that you were sore. What was he? Drunk?"

"Yes. Just a drunk," she said tightly. "Thank you, Casey. You were magnificent."

How could she tell him that he had just knocked down a vice cop? She only hoped that Crowley wouldn't try to find Casey, and she doubted that he would. Even a vice cop might have trouble about molesting a girl being escorted by the owner of a Montana business—a man as obviously respectable as Casey Shean.

But whatever the situation might be between Casey and Crowley, she had no doubts about her own status with Crowley. She had an enemy who could possibly make life untenable for her in the city.

She looked at Casey's strong profile as he watched the traffic and skillfully guided the car toward the outskirts of the city.

A feeling of warmth and affection crept through her. It was the first time a man had ever struck another man because of her; to protect her, to take care of her. It was a new, unusual and pleasant feeling of security. She never had felt quite like this before. She put a hand on his arm and sat a little closer.

"Really, Casey," she said. "You were wonderful. I just hope there'll be no trouble."

"There's nothing wonderful about an Irish temper," he smiled. "I don't think there'll be any trouble. Probably never see the guy again. I'll only be here until Saturday morning, and I don't think he'll come looking for me."

Ann fervently hoped he was right—that Crowley would not be looking for him. Casey patted the hand on his arm. "Anywhere you'd like to ride? It's your country. I don't know it too well."

"Just keep going," she smiled. "As long as you get me home by half past ten or so. I'm a working girl."

"I suppose a model has to get plenty of sleeep and watch herself," he nodded sagely. "I'll have you home by ten-thirty."

"And Casey—let's just drive?" she asked. "No parking. I—I don't want to talk any more. I mean, let's keep it like it is?"

"If you say so. I'm in no spot to be calling the plays, Ann. I'm simply glad to see you again and to be riding in a convertible with you. And maybe to be able to sock a drunk who gets fresh with you."

"Casey … pull up to the curb where it's dark under that tree."

He glanced at her, a little startled, and stopped the car in the darkness under the tree.

She turned to face him. She put her hand on his cheeks and looked deeply into his eyes. "I think I'd better kiss you," she said. "For being what you are. Here and now."

The kiss was unlike their kiss of greeting. He gave it a new intentness and hunger that she detected at once, and to which she found herself responding. She pushed him away. She couldn't let anything start, she warned herself. She had meant it to be only a kiss of thanks and affection born of nostalgia, but it hadn't turned out quite that way. It was time to run.

"Now let's go for our ride," she said almost primly, but tempering the words with a smile.

He laughed and started the car again. "How about tomorrow night?"

"I don't think so, Casey. I've other things already planned."

"Then the night after that?"

She shook her head. She musn't become too involved with him, and she had work to do. Nighttime was work time for her. She had to be realistic.

He drove in silence for a moment, his forehead creased with a frown. "I don't suppose—I mean you're probably busy. But I'm free tomorrow afternoon. How about it?"

She wondered if she dared.

"Maybe," she said. "For a little while."

"Fine. Let's make it tentative. Two o'clock?"

"All right. If anything comes up I'll call you," she said. She didn't want him to know about the answering service if he should call her, although he probably would think that it was because of her modeling jobs.

They rode leisurely, occasionally talking in short bursts of conversation. The night was pleasant, the traffic was light. She was glad they were not on the highway she had ridden the night before with Cal Marker. She wanted to forget Cal Marker, her life, and everything but Casey, the moment and the fact that there was another life outside "the life."

He delivered her to her apartment door precisely at ten-thirty.

"Tomorrow," he said firmly.

"I think so," she said. She looked up at him, prepared for his good night kiss.

He bent over and kissed her quickly. She had expected a harder, longer kiss, and the surprise must have shown in her eyes. He grinned and shook his head.

"A hallway ain't the place, ma'am! Not for how I seem to be feelin' about ye right now, ma'am. So I'll be after wishin' ye a pleasant good night!"

"You Irish Mick!" she laughed. "Go 'long with ye!"

"Not bad for a nonbeliever," he nodded gravely. "Tomorrow at two."

She didn't confirm the date. Tomorrow at two still was to be decided.

"Good night, Casey," she said softly. "And thanks—for everything."

After he was gone, she leaned back against her closed door and stared thoughtfully at the far wall of the room, unseeing and lost in thought.

She wasn't certain what had happened this evening, or of how she felt about Casey Shean. Strangely, she didn't want to think any more about it at the moment.

In a small gesture of resolution, she pushed herself straight from leaning back against the door and walked toward her bedroom. She had a date with a John in about twenty minutes. She would have to hurry.

Casey's remark about his former wife came to her mind again. *She might as well have been a whore.*

She smiled crookedly as she began to change clothes again.

"And *I* am, Casey!" she said aloud. "A whore."

CHAPTER FIVE

Her customer was waiting for her in a hotel suite. Men, she had discovered, could be typed. This one was large, black-haired, strongly featured, and a cigar smoker. His clothes were expensive. What luggage was visible was made of good leather. This was the heavy-handed big business man accustomed to ordering people around and to getting his way.

He sized up Ann with the same kind of look that he would have used in appraising a new car he was contemplating buying, or a thoroughbred dog, or a horse—if he liked blooded stock.

He was using a telephone when she knocked at the door. He called for her to come in, and he evaluated her with a deep searching look even as he still held the telephone in one hand, the fingers firmly cupped over the mouthpiece.

He nodded at Ann and indicated an open door with another nod. "The bedroom's in there," he said. "Get ready." He followed her across the room with his appraising eyes, his gaze centering finally upon the movement of her buttocks.

He removed the cupped hand from the telephone mouthpiece and spoke into the instrument. "All right, dear. I'll be back tomorrow afternoon on the three o'clock flight. Carl will pick me up at the airport and I'm going straight to the plant. But I'll be home in time for dinner."

He listened a few seconds and then said, "Yes. Everything's fine. I'll see you tomorrow, dear. Good night."

He put the instrument in its cradle, and through the open doorway—as she undressed—Ann watched him cross the room to a desk where a tray held bottles and glasses. He poured two drinks and brought them into the bedroom. He sat down on a chair and held out one of the drinks to her. She took it, even as she reached in back with her free hand to unfasten her brassiere. He watched her with appreciative eyes.

"You're a good-looking woman," he said bluntly.

"I'm glad you think so."

"Calman said I'd like you. Ann? Is that your name?"

"Yes. Ann Freeman."

He drank half of his drink and then bent over to untie his shoelaces. He had his suit jacket off and the French cuffs of his shirt were turned up loosely in a single roll. She saw his thick wrists and the black body hair. She knew that his body probably would be matted with that masculine, heavy hair. This was the all-man type, the big heman, the cave man.

Sex to him would be a vital, simple necessity. He would want it in the same way that he would want a heavy breakfast, a big lunch, and a meat-and-potato dinner. He was the driving, hard-working, hard-drinking, hard-living type. He would make money and be a success and manage lives. He knew what he wanted and how to get it, and accepted what he got as if he deserved all of it.

He stood and took off his shirt. He wore no undershirt. She knew instinctively that he would not. She saw the hair-covered chest that she expected. He finished undressing, quickly and without a trace of self-consciousness.

Ann went over to the bed and stretched out and waited. This was the way it would be with him. He knew what he wanted, directly and hungrily. There need be no subtleties nor wasted time on foreplay.

He came over and sat on the bed with his drink and smiled at her. "Did Calman suggest you do an especially good job to please me? I've been giving him a bad time."

She liked his bluntness and smiled. "He suggested something like that."

"I hope he added a little something extra to the fee," the man chuckled.

"Could be!"

He laughed and put down the drink beside the bed. "You'll earn it. I'm hungry."

"I *want* to earn it."

"Mind if I leave the light on?"

"Not at all."

He looked at her body again and nodded approval. "As my twenty-year-old son would say—you're stacked."

"And what would *you say*!" she asked coquettishly.

"I'd say you are a woman worth having—and I think it's time I did."

"Obviously," she said.

He was exactly as she thought he would be and she was tired when he finished with her. A fifty-dollar tip was in her purse when she left, and she suspected that she would receive an anonymous one hundred dollars through the mail within a day or so. This would be payment from Calman, and she was certain that her executive customer would give her a good report to warrant her the extra fifty dollars from Calman.

The lobby of the hotel was busy and she used a telephone booth to check her answering service. A smart girl never called from a customer's room. It was better to allow the customer the illusion of exclusiveness.

There was a number for her to call and she recognized it as Clara's. She glanced at her watch. It was almost one o'clock. Her recent customer had taken more time than she thought.

She dialed Clara's number and heard the low, husky voice of the statuesque brunette answer. Ann identified herself.

"Where are you?" Clara asked.

Ann told her.

"I'm glad I caught you," Clara said. "Marker's been trying to find you. He says for you to stay away from The Beard tonight. Crowley—that vice cop—has been there looking for you."

A small stab of concern brought a frown to Ann's face. She didn't want trouble with Crowley, and she didn't want Casey to have trouble. She wondered if she would have to expect Crowley hounding her from now on.

"I'll thank Cal when I see him," she said thoughtfully. "I had some trouble earlier tonight. I'll tell you about it later."

"Are you coming home?"

"I might as well. I haven't any calls. Are you through for the night?"

"Through and alone," Clara said, a tinge of anger in her voice. "I don't know where Mike is. I don't want to know. As a matter of fact I don't want to be here if and when he comes home tonight. I've had about all of Mike Lane I can take right now."

"He gives you a bad time," Ann admitted.

"Do you mind if I stay with you tonight, hon?" Clara asked. "Doesn't that studio couch make into an extra bed?"

"Come ahead," Ann said. "I'll be home in ten minutes or so. As soon as I can get a cab. We can have some coffee. I feel like talking, anyhow. We can both unload some troubles."

She hung up and left the booth, truthfully glad that Clara was going to spend the night with her. There were times when a girl had to talk, and if Clara had to do some talking, so did

Ann Freeman! Not that she would ever tell Clara too much. But there was the business about Crowley, and what she had better do about it all. Clara might have some good ideas, and she did have a few good contacts that might even cool Crowley a little.

She found a taxi and gave the driver her address. He looked at her in his rear-view mirror.

"Ain't I seen you on TV, Miss?" he asked.

"Possibly."

"Thought so. Never forget a face. Sort of a fetish of mine?"

"Fetish?"

"Yeah. I read up on psychology when things are slow. Like Freud and them guys. Like I got compulsions, too. Like when a smart punk tries to jockey me in traffic I got a compulsion to let him have it. Powie! Y'know?"

"I know," Ann smiled.

The driver kept up a running comment for the short ride to the apartment house and gave a friendly good night when she saw the size of her tip.

She checked the desk. There were no messages and she went up to her apartment and called Clara.

"I'm home," she announced. "You still want to stay with me?"

"Yes," Clara said in a short, angry voice. "I just got a line on Mike. He's with that damned young blonde chippie again. I'll be down."

Once in a great while another woman could cause Ann a certain uneasiness; a feeling of inadequacy; a small touch of inferiority complex.

Clara Lundy was one of those women, on occasion. Tonight was one of the occasions.

Ann had taken her usual long, cleansing bath and now she wore a shortie nightgown as she sat on the side of her bed watching Clara brush her black, glistening hair at a dressing table. Ann had refused to listen to Clara's suggestion about the studio couch, and Clara had not pressed it. Ann's bed was large and comfortable.

"Clara, how long have you been with Mike?" Ann asked suddenly.

The dark girl glanced up and her mouth set angrily. "It started about four years ago, Ann. Until then I wasn't really in the life. I was working the night club circuit, mostly as one of the girls. Sometimes—when things got tough—I did a little hustling. What the hell—I grew up in Detroit. My old man was Polish. My old lady ran off and left him with five of us kids. I was thirteen when that happened. When I was fourteen my old man started sleeping with me. I left home that winter. I never saw him again."

She put down the brush and swiveled around on the small bench at the table. She wore silk pajamas that accented the round, firm fullness of her large breasts, the tapered lines of her legs and thighs, and the richness of her woman's body.

Ann wondered if it was this full richness of body, the largeness of breasts, the long legs, the tallness, the statuesque proportions of the woman that sometimes brought her the uneasy feeling of inadequacy and even inferiority.

By comparison—and despite her own richness of body—she was smaller, and slimmer, and more feminine in a delicate way. Her breasts were young girl's breasts compared with the hard, jutting breasts of this full-bosomed, woman. Her thighs and hips were girlish compared with the rounded maturity of this black-haired woman.

Abruptly Ann realized that even as she was studying Clara's body and face, the other woman had been studying her with frank, appraising eyes. Ann had an odd desire to cover herself and she could almost feel an unusual blush of modesty.

She fought back the strange reaction. "Was there a man then?" she asked.

"No." Clara smiled. "There were men, but no man. I had a friend. A woman who was about thirty. She had a dance studio and I went there to learn to dance. She took me in and I lived with her for two years. She was killed in a car accident. After that I got jobs in clubs. I'd learned some dance routines. I even worked for a while as a stripper—they billed me as an exotic dancer. And then I met Mike."

"And got in the racket."

"It wasn't too hard. I was almost there. At first Mike talked about getting married—as soon as we had some dough so he could buy into a business deal. Sure. Me! I'd help. It was only for a few months. Mike was big that way. He understood. He knew I'd been sleeping around for money now and then. So before I knew it I was keeping him—and it's never changed."

She stopped speaking and shook her head.

"I mean until he got hooked," she continued. "But it's all over now, Ann. I know it. He's after this blond kid. He wants a stable. He asked me for my black book yesterday. You know what that means. He wants to get the kid started for him."

"Why don't you leave him?"

"Maybe that's why I'm here," Clara said. She looked into Ann's eyes and then turned back to the mirror and resumed her task with the hair brush. "Tell me why Crowley is looking for you."

Ann quickly told what had happened, leaving out the details of her former relationship with Casey and explaining him as an old friend of her youth. She did not want to discuss her actual feelings toward Casey with Clara. He was part of a life that had no place in the life she now led.

"Crowley's probably wild," Clara conceded. "Slugging a cop is violating all the commandments that weren't written. I hope he doesn't find your friend Casey."

"If he checks on Casey he may cool off. On the surface, Casey had every right to slug Crowley. It would look to anyone as if Crowley was annoying me. If he finds Casey and learns that he's legitimate, he'll probably drop it. Casey might make it rough for him."

"And if Casey is a guest at The Chateau, Crowley will think twice," Clara suggested. "That place carries weight in this town. They don't like to have guests annoyed. Even by vice cops."

Clara put down the brush and left the dressing table. She came around the bed and the two girls stretched out without pulling the sheet or light blanket over them. It was warm in the room.

"What are you going to do about Cal Marker?" Clara asked.

"Nothing," Ann said. "I'm not interested."

"He's plenty interested in you. A lot of the boys are. Sometimes I think Mike would be if he didn't know that you and I are friends like we are. He knows you wouldn't give him a look, and that I'd be gone for sure if he did." She held a hand up and inspected her highly lacquered nails. "I may be gone, anyhow. This blond kid—"

Clara turned on her side so that she faced Ann and propped herself upon one elbow as she looked down at the blond girl.

"You're a doll," she smiled, her dark eyes slowly traveling the length of Ann's body. "Tell me—have you ever been with a les?"

Ann felt uncomfortable again, and now she suspected why it might be. She knew that Clara never had objected to working a circus act with another girl, but she had considered it as probably a business arrangement with Clara. Other girls sometimes did. Sex was purely a commercial thing with them.

Clara had told a little too much, however. There had been the woman dance instructor in Detroit. The implication was clear. Not that it shocked Ann. A great many girls in the life were lesbians, even when they might have pimps. Some were bisexual in selection, enjoying either a man or another woman. It was quite possible that this could be true with Clara. It had just never occurred to her before, probably because Clara seemed to be so firmly attached to Mike. But now Clara was in revolt. She could be on a quiet hunt for some thing to substitute for Mike; preferably not another man.

Ann thought of these things while Clara continued to look at her and wait for the answer to her question.

"No." Ann admitted. "I've never been with a les."

Clara nodded. "I know you won't work a circus. But I wondered. It can be nice, you know."

Ann shut her eyes in confusion. This was the first time she had been directly approached by another woman, and she realized that the thought of it was more exciting than she would have believed possible. Or was it because she so seldom found any satisfaction with men?

"I don't know," she said honestly. "I've never thought much about it."

"You've been in the life long enough to know how common it is. You wouldn't be afraid of it, would you?"

"No, I don't think so."

She kept her eyes closed, not wanting to look into the other girl's face. She felt a slight movement on the bed and then, almost as lightly as the touch of a breeze, she felt Clara's hand caress the length of her bare thigh below the briefness of the shortie nightgown.

"You have a beautiful body," Clara said softly. "Do you like to have it stroked? Like this?"

Ann opened her eyes and looked up into the dark eyes. "Clara—are you a les? Is that it?"

"Sometimes—yes. I'm both. Now I want *you*. You see, I don't really *need* Mike. But I need someone to love. If you'll let me love you, we can both be happy. He can have his little blond bitch. I won't mind. And you won't need Marker or anyone. I'll look after you, Ann. I know how. I can do every thing for you."

"I don't know, Clara. I don't know if I'd like it. I've never done anything with another woman. Not that I don't understand. I'm in the life. I know. But—well, I just never tried it."

"It's really wonderful," Clara said softly. "Let me love you just a little. Tell me to stop if you don't like it."

Ann moved restlessly under the caressing hand and suddenly she knew that her discomfort and strange uneasiness with Clara was born of an unexplained and strangely intense desire.

"All right," she murmured. She shut her eyes again. "Just a little, Clara."

"Of course, darling. First, let's take off the shortie—"

Ann kept her eyes closed while the other woman removed the night garment. She heard Clara get up from the bed and the quick swish of silk and knew that she was removing her own pajamas. Then Clara's weight settled on the bed again and long, tapered, gentle fingers touched her intimately and skillfully.

Ann felt the tension leave her and a warm, delightful lassitude crept through her until she was limp and yielding, surrendering herself completely to Clara's practiced caresses. She felt soft, knowing lips on her breasts and belly and over the smooth, rounded columns of her thighs.

With infinite skill derived from experience, Clara employed a full repertoire of lesbian techniques until there could be no resistance in Ann—until Ann clutched Clara close to her trembling body and gave herself up to the warm flood of sensation that overwhelmed all her senses.

The night seemed to be without end. Clara was a resourceful exciting teacher. Ann became almost drugged with pleasure. Her inherent reticence to experience such intense intimacies with another woman was lulled into dormancy by Clara's persuasiveness. Ann suffered the exquisite suspense of the most delicate caresses, and surprised herself by giving them in return. This was like nothing she had ever known before, but even in its most profound depths of sensation she felt like a stranger in a foreign land. There was a feeling of guilt and revulsion—of enjoying the utterly forbidden—that became an unholy excitement in itself. There was the inclination to flee, yet she was fascinated and assailed by the lack of will to do anything but what was asked of her, in passive surrender, or in delicate attack.

The early gray light of false dawn was in the room when they finally slept, exhausted, intimately entwined together on the bed.

It was past noon when Ann awakened. She was fully awake in an instant, completely oriented to where she was and even, subconsciously to the time.

The night was etched vividly into her memory, and with the memory came a slight feeling of illness. She turned her head to see if Clara was with her. The bed beside her was empty. She sat up and looked into the living room through the open doorway. Clara was not in the other room. There was no sound in the apartment.

She glanced at a closet. The housecoat Clara had worn over her pajamas was gone. Evidently she had left. Ann threw back the sheet that Clara obviously had pulled over her and got up. There was a note on the dressing table.

I'll call you around 5 or 6—C.

Ann took a long, brisk shower, using a great deal of soap, and afterwards she carefully perfumed and powdered.

She refused to let herself think about the night before. She had experienced her first venture into the strange, perverted byways of lesbianism, and she hid from it now, avoiding her own evaluation of it as if she might find that she had liked the experience, when she did not want to like it, and already had felt a measure of regret.

She would think about it later. Now she would have coffee and a light breakfast. Casey would arrive at two o'clock if she didn't stop him.

Thoughtfully she dialed the answering service. There were no calls. She dropped the telephone into its cradle with a pensive, deliberate motion and stared at the instrument, thinking about Casey and wondering if she wanted to see him.

"I do," she thought. "At least once more."

She went to the kitchen to prepare coffee and toast. Her decision about Casey refused to be settled. There was a nagging, insinuating, persistent memory of what had happened with Clara. Finally, as she waited for her coffee, she faced the questions in her mind.

"All right," she told herself angrily. "Face it. You found a new low for yourself! You let her have her way and because you're a woman with the usual assortment of nerves and glands and sensory responses, you let her seduce you. Oh, you did it right, Ann! You let it get out of control and you abandoned yourself, and you even participated. You went all out—and got your lesbian kicks. Why? To prove what? That you're *not* a les like so many girls in the life are? The ones who are in *because* they are? Did you want to know if that's why you're what you are? Well, now you know. It didn't mean as much as Cal. Not even as much as Casey years ago. It's not for you. Never with a *woman*. Now you know and be thankful!"

She almost said the words aloud in her concentration and effort to know the truth about herself. The quick and definite conclusion satisfied her. Her decision about Casey was made now, too. She would see him. She wanted to see him. First there had been Marker. Then Clara. Now there might be escape back to a nebulous normalcy through Casey. She had to know. Somehow—and she didn't know why—she had a strange fear that time was running short. She had to learn quickly.

Casey arrived at two o'clock looking angry and worried despite his expansive smile. Ann had cocktails waiting, but he asked for straight whiskey with a water chaser before he took the more leisurely drink. He sprawled in an easy chair and looked at her quizzically.

"Our friend caught up with me around noon," he said.

Ann felt a chill of apprehension. "The man last night?"

"He's a vice cop. Ann, just what happened there?"

"I went to the powder room. When I was going back to our table he stopped me and … well, he accused me of being a girl looking for a pickup. I suppose he wanted to pick me up and got angry when I tried to get past him."

"He's a vice cop," Casey said. "He spotted me at the desk when I was checking on some business messages. There was the beginning of a real hassle until a hotel detective got in the act and checked on my being a guest and who I was. He leveled on the cop for bothering me—and any woman guest I had in the hotel."

"What did the vice cop say?"

"Obviously he had you confused with some girls around town. He said you are a known—well, do we need to go into that?"

"But Casey—!" *Oh, God*, she thought, *he knows.*

"I told him he was mistaken. He said if I knew who your friends are—something about a man named Marker—"

"Listen, Casey. He saw me with a man named Marker. That's true. But a girl in my business—" *What am I trying to do? Evade the truth? Lie? Why don't I admit it. This isn't for you. He isn't for you.*

"You don't have to explain anything to me, Ann," he interrupted. "So maybe you know some underworld characters. So what! I imagine any girl with a career in TV and modeling might meet people like that. I know a few myself. Some of my best friends on the golf courses have been professional gamblers. My first roommate at school, before I took the apartment, was a guy named Bill and one of my best friends for years. His mother once was a madam of a Butte whorehouse. So you meet people. You know people. That doesn't mean you're in business with them."

"Then you know I'm not—?"

"The cop made a mistake. Forget it. We smoothed it over. And that's it. Only I thought I'd let you know. If there's talk—you ought to know about it."

"Thanks, Casey," Ann said. Tears were very close to her eyes. The guy actually meant it. He didn't want her to prove anything; to defend herself; to refute Crowley. Obviously—and surprising to her in a world where she had become accustomed to acceptance of the worst—he simply didn't believe she could be a prostitute.

Casey still watched her, and he was smiling again. The smile erupted into a genuine small laugh. "You know," he said, "I'd certainly look like a chump—a first class square—if that cop were right. And do you know something else?"

"What Casey?"

"I've seen too many whores not to know one. I grew up in a tough town. I knocked around in tough places. Sure. I've been with prostitutes—you know about one. I told you years ago. And others since. Enough that I'd *know* one, and know when a girl *isn't* one! You'd have the look, Ann—and, of course, you don't."

Oh, Casey—you poor fool. You poor dear fool with your strange Irish faith in the goodness of people. With your sentimental eyes for a girl you used to sleep with in a back room during a university school term. Don't you know how times change? They're packaging sex in deluxe models now—educated, cultured, smart, sophisticated, svelte, smooth, and select. Like me. But thank you for believing!

"Casey—was there anything special you wanted to do this afternoon. I have until about six. I've a car in the basement. Would you like to drive?"

"Whatever you'd like to do."

"I know a place," she said. "It's on a small river where we can swim. And the day is beautiful. It would take us less than an hour to get there. We could stop somewhere and buy you swim trunks on the way."

"It's a deal!"

Then, almost magically, the day took on a holiday mood. Ann offered him the keys to her car, but he insisted that she drive. They stopped at a sports store and bought him swim trunks and at a liquor store he bought wine.

"Warming after a swim, if the water's cold," he explained gravely.

She drove swiftly over a secondary highway into mountain country and finally turned into a paved feeder highway that took them into the valley where the river flowed.

She turned into a road that apparently led to a rambling old farmhouse. A homemade sign read: PICNIC GROUNDS— SWIMMING—$1.00 A CAR. Ann sounded the car horn and an old man came out of the house. He grinned a welcome and took the dollar bill Casey offered him.

"You're the only ones today, folks," he told them. "You'll have the beach all to yourself. Ain't likely anyone'll be around. Mostly they come weekends."

He motioned vaguely toward the dirt road that led downward through trees toward the river. Ann drove slowly and after a short time she parked in shade and got out.

"The river's right down there," she said. She found a folded blanket in the trunk compartment and they left the car and walked down the wooded slope until suddenly they were upon a smooth expanse of white beach and the surprisingly wide river that drifted slowly around a large bend.

The beach was isolated. No houses or highway was in sight, and back from the beach there was a grotto surounded by trees and carpeted by soft grass.

"I'll change in there," she decided. "You can go down-stream behind those bushes." She took the blanket into the grotto and spread it on the grass. She realized then that she had not brought towels. They would have to dry in the sun. Casey had given her the wine and she found a shaded place for it, wondering if it would become too warm. Perhaps they could cool it in the water.

They went into the water together. It was pleasantly warm and they swam slowly and easily. There was no need to talk, and nothing to talk about.

Afterwards they stretched out on the blanket to dry. Casey opened the wine and they drank from the bottle. They lay on their backs and looked up at the deep blue sky and listened to the sounds of the river and insects and birds. The smell of evergreens was in the air, and the closeness of grass and clover was rich in fragrance.

Ann shut her eyes and wondered if she had known such a peaceful, restful, contented moment in years. The mountain river water had cleansed her with its freshness; the air was soft and perfumed with the scent of moist earth and growing things; and the warmth of good wine was tingling through her body.

She realized that Casey had moved and that he was close to her. She opened her eyes and she was looking directly up into his face as he leaned over her, even as Clara had leaned over her only a few hours ago, only it seemed now that it must have been a lifetime ago in another age.

"Maturity becomes you," Casey said softly. "You're more beautiful—more lovely than ever. I'm glad I looked for you."

"I'm glad, too, Casey," she whispered. She reached up a hand and idly traced the line of his jaw as she once had done in the quiet of a small room years before. "It becomes you, too. Maturity. Manhood. Are you happy, Casey?"

"In some ways. My work, the plant, what I'm doing with myself—yes, I'm happy about that. My independence—I guess I'm happy about that. Or maybe it's being happy for freedom from an unhappiness that I had for a while."

"You make it sound complicated. Either you're happy or you're not," she smiled.

"Then right now I'm happy. I'm going to kiss you. It's called for, I think."

"Yes, it's called for, I think," she agreed. She shut her eyes and felt the slow, even pressure of his lips. It was not a hard and demanding kiss such as she she had learned to avoid so adroitly, nor the deep and insinuating one, that she so often turned away. It was a gentle, full, and *caring* kiss. That was the only word she could think of for it. *Caring.* And it was good to be cared for, to have someone care for you.

After a time he drew away from her.

"I'd better stop it," he smiled quizzically. "I made a mistake once. Back in Missoula. I don't want to make it again. I lost you that time."

She looked up at him, strangely content to shake her head as if she objected to his drawing away from her. She reached a hand to his face.

"Come back," she said. "It's all right."

"We're not kids any more, Ann."

"All the more reason."

"I know. But last night—this morning—this afternoon I've been thinking about us. I'm not sure. Maybe you've changed too much to be interested. I don't know you any more, or if I'd measure up. Your life has probably been exciting. Modeling. TV. I know I'm not in orbit with that sort of thing. But—"

He stopped talking as if he had run out of words and had to regroup his thoughts and build new phrases.

"Maybe," he said thoughtfully. "Maybe I'm trying to think of us being married. Maybe I'm trying to admit that I never quite got over it through the years. Maybe I've never wanted anyone but you."

"Maybe you're just imagining things," she smiled, not quite believing herself and knowing that what she heard was sweet to hear.

The warmth of sun and wine made her drowsy. There was contentment and escape in Casey's voice, in his words, and in his very presence.

"Come back," she said again, lazily, her eyes half closed. She slid her hand behind his neck and pulled him down to her.

For a few seconds she felt the even, full pressure of his lips on hers again, and then she opened her lips and gave him the fullness of the deep kiss that had been withheld.

She felt his arms tighten and the quick, certain rise of his desire. She felt his fingers fumble with the straps of her bathing suit and she dropped her arms from around him and held them close to her sides so that the straps slipped down over her shoulders and elbows and hands. With eyes still closed she lifted herself while he tugged at the garment, and then she felt the release from the fabric and the freedom of the soft summer breeze upon her naked body.

"It's all right," she whispered. "It's all right, Casey."

Moments later she rested in his arms, opening her eyes for a few moments as he held her, gently conquered, in the brief pause of adjustment.

"I love you, Ann," he said. "I mean it."

She simply smiled and shut her eyes and moved tentatively so that he held her more closely and urgently. Then his eager, insistent lips roved from her mouth to the soft planes and curves of her body, lingering for a long time on her firm breasts while desire quickened in her, heating up all the fibers of her loins.

For a few moments, and only moments, she was back again in the room in Missoula. The movements, the murmured words and excitement were singularly Casey's. Then they were every man's, as she knew. Then—because he was tenderly fierce, and fiercely tender—she was thankful that she could give him this brief span of happiness and she joyfully employed all the lore of love making that she had learned. She deliberately and ecstatically brought him to breathless culmination, glorying in her ability to do so, and strangely startled and deeply excited when she realized that she would join him in the peak of his ecstasy.

"It's good," she thought. "Good ..."

Casey cried out with a masculine sound of achievement and capture. Then he was quiet except for his heavy breathing and a gentle fumbling of lips upon her mouth.

"Thank you, Ann—thank you."

"I know," she whispered. "Oh, Casey ... I *know.*"

Later, as they rested in the sun, he tried to talk about it.

"Ann, I don't want you to think that I just wanted—"

"I don't," she interrupted. Now that it was over, she didn't want to talk about it or think about it. She had the feeling that she had given a gift. She didn't want effusive thanks.

Although she had experienced a magnificent and thrilling emotional satisfaction, in retrospect, it seemed almost that she had achieved it for herself. Somehow during the moments of communion she had taken the ascendancy from him, and had shaped the interlude to her own pattern.

Now it was done. She wasn't certain what she felt for Casey. There was a nostalgia. There was a deep appreciation for his faith in her, and his tenderness, and his obvious desire. But she felt a lack of some essential element.

Deliberately she thought about herself. She recalled the previous night and her experience with Clara. That had been an experiment, and she had found it lacking.

The men she had been with—the Johns—over the last two days had meant little or nothing as usual.

If there was a comparison to be made, she knew that it was inspired by Cal Marker. Even the thought of him now brought deep disturbances of emotions and physical excitement.

Involuntarily she reached out a hand and found one of Casey's as if she sought quick protection from danger. She pushed Cal Marker from her thoughts.

"Casey," she said. "We have to go. Let's not talk about it any more. Not now. It was good and—let's just leave it at that for the time being. All right?"

"I'm going home Saturday."

"Nothing has to be decided by then. Maybe there is nothing to *be* decided, Casey. This is just an afternoon in the right place at the right time, and we *did* have something nine years ago. We had to find out."

"It was never so good then," he smiled. "You're beautiful, perfect, wonderful. You're all the Irish adjectives a man ever used for a woman."

"Blarney gets you nowhere!" she laughed and sat up. She reached for clothing neatly folded near the edge of the blanket beside the hastily-cast-aside bathing suit. "Come on, Irish. We have to go."

"Ann, tell me. Was it really good for you?"

"Yes. Really good. But that isn't an answer to anything. Please, Casey—don't think that it is."

CHAPTER SIX

They were back in town by five-thirty and despite Casey's urging that she have dinner with him, she refused and let him out at The Chateau.

Things were becoming too complicated for her, she thought. Cal Marker. Clara, and Casey Shean had intruded forcibly into her life within a short span of hours. Mike Lane was interested in her now because he was trying to build a stable, and maybe he had seen Marker's obvious desire for her. And in the background there was the ominous figure of a vice cop named Crowley.

Meanwhile the high rent continued—the answering service, the expensive way of life had to be paid for. She had to work.

She settled for a hamburger and coffee at a drive-in on the outskirts of town and then drove to the apartment house. It was six-thirty when she entered her apartment and checked with the answering service. She had had three calls, two of them regular customers, and a third recommended by another.

With a little diplomatic arranging she was able to set up the dates over the evening with plenty of time between each. One was at seven-thirty and it would not be strenuous. Dil Clay, middle-aged and wealthy, considered to be one of the most eligible bachelors in the city had been seeing her about once every two weeks for a year and a half.

She bathed quickly and was dressing to keep her date with him when the door chime sounded. She went to the door to admit Clara.

"I called several times," Clara said. "I thought you'd be in. Didn't you get my note, hon?"

"Casey and I went for a swim," Ann said, returning to the small task of putting on lipstick. She was dressed in a robe, over black lace panties and brassiere. The black lingerie had been given to her by Dil Clay with the request that she wear the garments when she visited him.

She looked at this tall, dark woman who had made love to her the night before and understood why men could become excited about her. Even as a woman might. If there was a universal embodiment of all sex in one person, it certainly was evident in Clara Lundy.

"Did Mike come home?" Ann asked carefully, wanting to turn the conversation away from the previous night.

Clara crossed the room and sat on the side of the bed. She wore a smart outfit that would have cost at least $300 retail, but had been hers for a fraction of its value through the old man in his single room.

"He's home. He was there when I went up this morning."

"And?" Ann began to use a small smount of eye makeup.

"It isn't so bad now, Ann. I mean, he doesn't bug me like he did. I don't care so much. Know what I mean?"

Ann didn't answer.

"Now that you and I have what we have," Clara said significantly, "I don't need him like I did. So he takes care of some of my problems. He takes care of the fuzz if I fall. He sees I have nothing to worry about. I don't mind now. I don't need him for the other. I mean—so he takes on that little blond chippie. Let him. She's strictly from nothing. A hustler. I'm still head chick because I'm still his star. He needs me—but now I don't need him. I've got *you*."

Ann finished her make up and stood and took off the robe to get into a frock for the evening. Clara stared at her, obviously excited by the sudden sight of the smaller, blond girl in the black lingerie of Dil Clay's selection; the single, diaphanous Bikini-styled silk garment at the hips and the transparency of the bra.

In a smooth movement that was so sudden that Ann was completely unprepared for it, Clara stood and came to her and took her into a close, demanding embrace.

"Girl," Clara murmured. "You're my girl."

Ann pushed away from her. She didn't know how she was going to handle this. She felt a deep and understanding compassion for Clara. She understood how Clara was trying desperately to adjust to the fact that she might be losing a precious exclusiveness to the man she was keeping. For Clara there was a loss of caste, of stature, of self-esteem, of security in the fact that Mike Lane was looking for other women to help support his dope habit.

"Don't," Ann said gently. "Please don't, Clara. And try to understand. You're wrong. I'm not your girl. You don't have me— not that way. As a friend, but not the other."

"I know," Clara said soothingly. "It can be that way the first time. You're not sure, but I can make you sure, baby. Let Clara make it certain for you. Right now. We have time."

Ann drew away from the taller woman, avoiding the caressing hands. "Please, Clara. Last night happened, but I'm not that way. I'm not a les. Not really."

"Don't say that, darling. Remember how it was with us. Don't you see? I'm really leaving Mike for you. He won't mean anything to me except in the racket. His contacts. But that's all."

"No, Clara."

Clara was staring at her intensely, her nostrils flaring a trifle, and her breathing quickened. She made a motion toward Ann again.

"Listen, hon—maybe I'd leave Mike," she said. "I'd take care of you instead. I can hustle enough for both of us. You wouldn't have to turn any more tricks. Just be my girl."

"God damn it, don't talk that way!" Ann said desperately and a little annoyed. "I don't want any of it, Clara. I don't want to hurt you, but you've got to understand. Go back to Mike. Or find another girl. I like you. You're my friend. But not that way. I'm not a les. I'm not looking for a bull dyke. Is that clear?"

"You liked it well enough last night," Clara said in a quiet level voice that held an edge of anger. "And you were giving as good as you were getting."

"All right! You've said it. Last night was last night. That was it. There's no more."

For a few seconds the tall, dark woman looked angry enough to slash at the smaller girl, but she managed to control herself, and she smiled thinly.

"You'll change your mind, baby," she said. "You've had a taste of it and you'll want more. You'll want Clara."

Ann got into the frock she was going to wear, feeling safer with the additional clothing. She didn't want to quarrel with Clara, and she didn't want to hurt the other woman.

"Look, Clara, I have to run. I've a John waiting for me."

"Will you be at The Beard later?"

"I don't know. I'm booked solid tonight."

"I'm meeting Mike there after midnight. But I'll come home with you."

"No, Clara."

The tall girl laughed softly and shook her head. "Don't fight it, baby. Not after last night. I *know!*" She surveyed the blond girl with a critical eye and nodded approval. "You look wonderful in that. I'll see you later." She walked leisurely out of the bedroom, crossed the living room, and let herself out of the apartment with a backward glance and wave.

Ann frowned at the closed door.

Dil Clay's apartment was in the most exclusive residence building in the city. The decor reflected an Oriental influence. His bedroom was masculine in accent, but unusual in taste.

There was a large, black, teak bedstead with a black silk spread. The carpet of the room was white. One wall was a picture window with a glass panel doorway to a balcony that overlooked the city. The three remaining walls were wood-paneled except for large, built-in mirrors. Ann knew from experience that the mirrors were focused upon the bed, and that there were controlled lighting effects.

Dil Clay, thin, slightly gray at the temples, and debonair in a black robe of Oriental cut, sat in a low teakwood chair and watched Ann slowly remove the frock and then stand before him in the diaphanous undergarments he had purchased for her.

She moved slowly and deliberately. Soft music flowed into the room from concealed speakers. The illumination in the room was subdued except for a discreet highlight upon the black bed.

For a moment she stood posed before him in the black silk, and then she deliberately removed the garments and walked to the bed. She lay back, her finely molded body white in contrast against the black silk.

Dil Clay had risen now from the chair and he crossed the room and returned with a singularly high chair of straight, Chinese design. He placed the chair at the foot of the bed where it towered at about the height of a draftsman's stool. Clay sat on the chair and looked down at the girl.

"I am an emperor and you are a slave girl," he said. "I've sent for you. Now I want to see if you have learned your lessons well and know how to please me. Show me how you will move to arouse me and then to satisfy me."

This was the game they played. Ann knew the psychiatric names for the strange impulses that controlled some men's perverted desires. There were the voyeurs who liked to look, the scoptophiliacs, the fetishists, the exhibitionists, the sadists, the masochists. There were others with strange and weird desires too complex to understand. And there was Dil Clay with his imagination and strange compulsions.

"Watch yourself in the mirrors, slave girl," he commanded. "See that you show me well."

In fifteen minutes it was finished. Clay paid her with crisp new banknotes, looking subdued and ashamed.

"Thank you, Ann," he said. "I'm glad you understand."

"I know," Ann smiled. She had no feeling of revulsion or dislike about this man. He was a good customer, and his compulsions and desires were not of his making. If she served him well without feeling his touch, nor any bodily contact, and only by playing part of his game for him, this, too, was her job.

"I'll call you," he said as she left.

She had coffee at a drugstore counter between dates. She knew exactly where she was going, and the customer was a regular. He would supposedly be working late in a richly appointed office suite where his name was on the president's office door.

There would be a friendly drink, which he would not really want, but would believe was necessary for them. He would ask her politely about her health. He would discuss this briefly, all the time watching her with the hunger slowly gathering in his eyes as he looked at her outlined breasts and the tightness of skirt over hips and thighs.

He was a rather short, precise-looking man with a tightly cut mustache. His wife's name was frequently in the society pages. His name was occasionally mentioned in business and news magazines.

After the drink he would smile briskly and say, "Well, Ann?"

She would smile and they would leave the office and go into the small adjoining room that had a private bathroom and a discreet leather couch where the executive could rest upon occasion.

Ann would undress quickly while he spread a blanket over the cold leather of the couch. He would take one of the large bath towels from the bathroom and spread it over the blanket.

Thus were the mechanics of expensive prostitution managed. And there—behind locked doors, with the lights turned out—the brisk, important, efficient corporation president would have her, taking his fill of her lush, yielding, naked flesh. He was always eager, sometimes frantic with her but never rough or savage. She suffered the caresses of his carefully manicured hands and occasionally permitted him to kiss her. To him it would be a brief and most pleasant interlude that made living with a frigid wife more bearable. To Ann it would be a quick trick for fifty dollars with a regular customer.

She smiled as she thought about it at the drugstore counter. The coffee was hot and she sipped it slowly. A well-dressed young man came into the store, glanced at her and sat one stool away. He ordered coffee and smiled at her.

She ignored him. In the mirror of the back bar she saw him watching her. He turned sideways on the stool as if to look out of the store window at the street. She was directly in his line of vision. He looked at her profile, her breasts, her legs.

Without glancing at him she finished her coffee, paid her check, and left the store. She found a taxi at the next corner and gave the address of the office building where the corporation president would be waiting....

At eleven o'clock, after she had left the office building and the corporation president, she tapped lightly on a hotel door and an advertising account executive, in town on a business trip, with a lenient expense account, let her in.

The date had been set up easily when she had called the hotel number he had left and asked for "Mr. Sands in 509."

A pleasant, cultured voice had answered.

"I'm Ann Freeman," she had said.

"Oh, yes. We have a mutual friend here. Ralph Kittridge."

"Yes. I know him quite well. You're an advertising friend of his?"

"From out of town. Sort of a visiting account executive. I expect to finish my business early this evening and take an early morning plane out. It's so seldom I get away from home—I thought perhaps—"

"Did Mr. Kittridge have any suggestions?"

"Oh, yes. Very definite. He also mentioned something about fifty."

"It's a nice number," she had said. "Say at eleven?"

"That would be excellent."

So now it was eleven o'clock and a rather good-looking man in his thirties was inviting her into his two-room hotel suite. He was of medium height, build, and weight. His hair was cut in the Madison Avenue version of the crew cut. An attaché case was open on a desk with several sheafs of paper visible. In one corner of the small living room a television set was turned on.

"Come in, Ann," Sands said hurriedly. "I want to catch the commercial on this break."

He indicated a chair for her and then turned his attention to the television screen. A commercial for beer came on. Sands gave it his concentrated attention, and snapped off the set when it was finished.

"We're interested in that account," he explained to Ann, sizing her up with interested eyes as he spoke. "Kittridge was right."

"I hope that means what I think it does," Ann smiled.

"Drink?" he asked, indicating a bottle and glasses on a table.

"Not unless you want one."

"I've had all I want. I can think of more pleasant things to do."

"Shall we?"

"With pleasure!"

"I'm certain—with pleasure!" Ann smiled as she preceded him into the bedroom.

A few moments after midnight she paid off a taxi in front of The Beard.

She had hesitated about going there after leaving her last customer, but she felt a reluctance to avoiding Clara or Mike or Cal Marker. It was too much like running away, and it would only be a postponement of the issue. The sooner she got things settled, the better it would be, and an open attack and exposure was the most effective way of doing it.

She crossed the poorly lighted street and went into the club. The place was filled and the combo was well warmed up to its progressive jazz.

She began to thread her way toward the bar when a hard hand clamped on her arm.

Ann turned in annoyance. Some men—!

"I've been looking for you," Crowley said. "Let's take a little ride."

CHAPTER SEVEN

Ann felt blood drain from her face. A cold knot was centered in the pit of her stomach, and she knew that she couldn't speak if she tried.

This was the dreaded moment. Since she had begun to live "the life" she had known that someday there would be a moment when a police officer would put a hand on her arm and flash a badge.

Some day she would stand before a judge to face the charge of prostitution in whatever legal language they would couch it. But the first moment in that sequence of devastating events would be the moment when a policeman arrested her.

Sometimes she had planned what she would do and say. She had pictured the attitude she might take. She had thought of things to say, of excuses to give, of denials. She would keep her poise. She would summon all the years of rearing in a good middle-class family, the background of the university, the indignant anger; the cold, cutting words that an innocent, decent woman would use.

When that moment came she would not allow herself to translate what was happening into the language she had learned to use. It would be a *police officer*, and not a roller, or nailer, or the fuzz. It would be an *attempted arrest*—not a fall or a bust. She would refuse to understand or acknowledge the words the arresting officer might use. She would scorn the four-letter words for intercourse, the improper language for clinical description. She would resist with aloofness, and be above what the world said she actually was.

This is what she had told herself.

Now the moment was here and she looked up into the face of the vice squad man and she couldn't speak. She never had been so frightened, nor so hopelessly sick of what she had become.

Finally she managed to speak. Her voice sounded strange in her own ears; tense, hoarse, uncertain.

"I don't understand," she protested. "What do you mean?"

"Knock it off, girlie. You know what I mean. There's an ordinance about soliciting."

"You didn't see me solicit anyone—not even talk with anyone since I've come in here! You can't—"

"I can," Crowley said briefly. "Because I'm the man you propositioned. You asked me to take you for a ride in my car. And for ten bucks you'd mke it interesting. And we went. You showed that you meant business as soon as we were parked around the corner in that vacant lot. You pulled up your dress and pulled off your pants. And that's when I flashed my badge."

He had pulled her into the small foyer of the club. No one noticed them in the poorly lit entrance, busy with the coming and going of people. The combo was loud, the music drowning conversation.

"Damn you—let me go!" Ann tried to slap the heavy face. Crowley laughed and his hand crushed on her arm until she winced with pain.

"Outside," he snapped. "Now."

She went with him because the pain of his gripping hand was too great for her to resist; because no one was there to help her; because there was no use in screaming because a cop was arresting her; nor in protesting when there was no one to listen.

It was not a police car, but obviously his own. He made her go to the street side and slip under the wheel to the opposite side so that he could retain his grip on her arm as he got behind the wheel.

He started the car and drove a half block and wheeled into the darkness of a deserted parking lot. He stopped in darkness beside a building.

"No," Ann said. "You can't. You're framing me. You can't get away with this."

"I didn't like you from the beginning," he said softly, intensely. "And I didn't like getting clipped by that John you had. He almost caused me some trouble. So I'm going to even it up— show them what you are; let you take the rap you've got coming."

"What kind of a cop are you?" Ann asked plaintively, trying a new tactic. "Cops aren't supposed to act like—like—"

"You can knock that off, too, girlie. Save it for the kid rookies, the college boys. Me—I'm from the old school, and I've got a lousy reputation. You can't hurt it any. They might believe you, but they won't admit it because I'm still a cop, and because you can't prove anything. Even if they wish you could so they could dump me."

Ann pulled back from him into the far corner of the car seat. "I didn't ask that guy to hit you," she said. "It was an accident. He didn't know. Don't blame me for his temper."

"Try again, baby. That isn't good enough."

She took a deep quivering breath. "Would fifty dollars be good enough?"

"Let's see it?"

With trembling fingers she brought out the fifty dollars she had received from Sands. She started to hand it to Crowley, but he snatched it from her fingers and took the small handbag she carried. He opened it and took the remaining hundred dollars she had earned during the night, along with what other money she had with her.

"So you're a star?" he grinned. "Who's your old man? Marker?"

"No."

"Mike Lane."

"No. I don't have one. You can't prove anything. I'm not a prostitute."

"So she's not a prostitute!" he grinned. "She uses nice language. She's educated!"

He tossed the purse on the floor and reached for her. She tried to get out of the car, but he caught her with the bruising hands and pulled her back.

"Let's set the record straight, girlie. If you want to use your education, you're a prostitute. You're also a hooker, call girl, street walker, hustler, white meat, and whore. Now we're going to get out of this front seat and get in the back seat and you're going to prove it."

"No. Damn you, let me alone!"

He laughed as she tried to fight him. He reached around and opened the car door and shoved her out so that she fell to the asphalt surface of the parking lot. He was beside her before she could get up. He jerked her to her feet and shoved her through the opened back door of the car. He climbed in after her and pulled the door shut.

"Remember what I said?" Crowley breathed. "About pulling up your dress? Well—let's get at it, girlie. Let's make it legitimate."

Ann tried to escape with a wild struggle. She felt herself crushed back against the seat and the man's knee pried between her legs. His hand clawed at the hem of her skirt.

Suddenly Crowley was jerked backwards. He uttered a startled half-strangled oath. By the time Ann had struggled up from the seat cushion, Crowley was out of the car, face down on the asphalt.

He tried to get up and the man over him helped him and then chopped a slashing blow with the side of his hand upon Crowley's shoulder as the detective tried to pull a gun.

"Don't do it, you son-of-a-bitch," Cal Marker warned.

Ann stared at him in the half light of the parking lot. Marker had lost his Ivy League look, and there was a tense, hard, competent toughness about him.

Crowley snarled: "You damned pimp, I'll kill you!"

He sprang at Marker in a violent onslaught of battering fists. The men collided and went down.

Marker rolled sharply to get away from the vicious fists, jolting short, hard blows into Crowley's face. The cop shook off the blows in angry indifference that seemed to make him immune to pain, and to forget the gun holstered under his coat.

He jabbed straight fingers at Marker's eyes, but the lighter man managed to break free and evade the blinding fingers. The men scrambled to their feet and circled warily.

"I'll get you," Crowley breathed hoarsely. "Now!"

He came in again, swinging low, crashing blows into Marker's body, Marker grunted and lashed out with a fist that split Crowley's lips.

The blow increased Crowley's fury. He rushed again with harsh, biting oaths accenting his hammering fists.

Marker side stepped and clamped both hands upon one of Crowley's thick wrists, turned, bent, and whipped the body of the bulkier man over a shoulder. Crowley hit the pavement with a crunching thud.

The detective shook his head and slowly got to his feet. His eyes were wide with frustrated rage. His shoulders were hunched in fury that demanded action.

"You asked for it," he spat from bleeding lips. "By God, you asked for it. Resisting arrest."

He reached for his gun again. His intention was obvious. Ann screamed a frantic warning.

Marker saw the danger. He brought an arm up and down in that angry hatchet chop. The side of his hand brought a howl of pain from Crowley as the blow temporarily paralyzed his gun arm.

Marker smiled without humor. "You're a lousy cop or I couldn't do that," he said. "It's been a hell of a long time since I was in the service. A good cop would out-judo me. But not you."

"I'm going to fix you for this!"

"You're going to forget all about it," Marker said. "You know Jerry Delake. You know what he can do with a good case in any court. So if you want to do anything more about this, you're going to have Jerry Delake defending this chick, and you're going to be up for attempted rape among other things. She's got a witness. I've been standing in the shadows behind that post for ten minutes."

Crowley glared at the younger man.

Marker smiled again. "That's the way it is, roller. You're up against a tough mouthpiece. A rap for rape. To say nothing of the dough you took out of her purse—and the whole, stinking goddamned frame you tried to work. You want to put up your lousy word against all of that? Hell. Even the fuzz wish they could get rid of you. And *I* have ever since they transferred you. You've been on my back. Now you can get off. But good."

It was an unusually long speech for Marker, but he seemed to enjoy it and when he was finished he put an arm around Ann and held her against him. "You okay, baby?"

"Yes," she stammered. She was shaken and weak.

"How much did he take from you?"

"A little over a hundred and fifty."

Marker held out his hand. "Give, cop. It doesn't belong to you. And don't reach for the gun. You've got enough trouble. I don't want to use any more judo. I might make a mistake. Guys have been killed that way."

Crowley carefully pulled the money from a side coat pocket and handed it to Marker who gave it to Ann. "Check it," he said.

Almost indifferently Ann glanced at the money.

"It's here," she murmured.

Marker reached forward and took the vice man's gun from a shoulder holster and threw it across the lot. "Okay," he said to Ann. "Let's go. We've all had it for tonight."

This time Marker did not wheel the low, sleek Jag over a country highway, but drove it through streets and into the basement garage of a towering apartment building.

They spoke little during the short ride. He explained that he had witnessed Crowley's actions at the club and had followed them. She thanked him, but he silenced her with a shrug and grin.

"Later, baby," he said.

In the basement he parked the car and led the way to an automatic elevator. They rode up to the tenth floor and walked into a heavily-carpeted hallway. He took out a key and unlocked a door. Ann walked into an apartment and looked around with appreciation of the decor.

"My pad," he said. "Like?"

"It's beautiful," she acknowledged.

"And expensive. It's the way I like to live." He mixed drinks for them at a small bar while she went to the luxuriously appointed bathroom and repaired the damage Crowley had done to her make up and clothing. She glanced at a glass-enclosed shower and her obsession for cleanliness overcame her. She went back to the living room.

"Cal, do you mind if I take a shower?"

He brought her a drink. "Not at all. I think there's an extra robe in a closet." He went into a bedroom and returned with a white silk robe. She draped it over an arm, catching a faint fragrance of perfume from the garment. Some other woman had worn it, and not too long ago. She wondered if any of his women lived with him.

He seemed to read her mind. "I live alone," he smiled.

She took a long refreshing shower. For a moment she considered putting on her clothes again, but remembered the scene at the parking lot and what Cal Marker had done for her. If he wanted her to come out to him with nothing on but the robe, she certainly owed him that much.

She was not surprised to find him dressed in pajamas and a robe in the living room. He had mixed fresh drinks for them and a radio was softly filling the room with music.

"Come here," he said quietly, indicating the couch where he sat.

Obediently she went to him and took the drink he offered. She sat back, modestly pulling the opening of the robe together above her knees. He looked at her with approving eyes and nodded.

"I like a chickie who's a star," he said. "We can make it together."

"Cal, I owe you for tonight. I know it. Believe me. But I won't be one of your cows."

"Who the hell said you'd be a cow, baby? Look—you'll be head chick. The others don't mean anything to me. You think I'd brace Crowley like that tonight if I didn't make it big for you?"

"No, Cal. I guess not."

"What would you have done, baby? The arm was on you. You were taking a fall. More than that—remember your dough, and everything else he was going to take from you. And once you'd been booked, you'd be marked as an easy collar for any cop who needed to fill a quota. You've had no protection. You've had nobody taking care of things for you. But you do now. You've got me."

She finished her drink, trying to tell herself that he was wrong; that a girl could handle things alone if she stayed smart. But she remembered the panic of the moment when Crowley's hand had fallen on her. She wasn't sure.

"Let me think, Cal. I'm tired. I'm mixed up."

"Sure, baby. That's what I want you to do. Think. We're going to bed now. You don't have to worry. You can think about it in the morning. Right now you're my baby. My head chick. I'll show you how it'll be, baby. From now on."

She looked into his eyes, and there was no refusing. She had come here with him. She owed him something. More than that— suddenly she *wanted* him. Tomorrow could take care of itself, and tomorrow the questions could be answered, but right now, this moment, all of the answers to every question in her mind would be answered when she was in his arms.

He got up and in an easy gesture he stooped and picked her up. The robe fell open and she made no movement to close it. He didn't bother to turn off the radio nor turn out the lights as he carried her from the room. In the bedroom he put her down on his bed.

He turned on a soft light and took off his robe and pajamas. Once again she was conscious of his lean, athletic body. She remembered the way he had handled Crowley, and she saw the sinews and muscles and smooth, quick strenth of the arm that had chopped so effectively.

131

She wondered what had made him what he was now. Men who weren't as good-looking, nor as well built and effective of body, nor as intelligent—as she was certain he was—became business executives, engineers, pilots, lawyers, politicians, cops, salesmen, mechanics, leaders. What had made Cal Marker become a pimp?

Or was that the right word? It didn't fit this man, even when she knew it was true.

He hung his robe and pajamas in a closet and left open the panel of the built-in closet as he came toward the bed.

Ann's excitement was deep and frantic again. Nothing had changed from the experience of the other night, unless it was an increased intensity because now she felt that she owed him herself; that he had bought her with protection.

For a moment he stood motionless by the bed, looking down at her, quietly smiling, and deliberately enjoying her as he might a painting, or a statue or any beauty of line and substance.

She saw the dominance of male desire in his face, and she closed her eyes and waited for the first caress of his hand or lips.

At the moment it seemed that this awaited caress was the full deliverance from the loveless childhood she had known, that she existed solely to satisfy Cal Marker's need, his hunger, his desires. In his eyes and facial expression she had seen the one thing she once had desired more than anything: the knowledge that someone wanted her and needed her.

She felt a deep desire to thank him for protecting her and wanting her, and the desire became translated into the welcoming movements of her body.

His hands were upon her and she smiled. She felt her own involuntary response and was pleased when she knew that he had found her movements exciting and to his liking.

His lips asserted intimate demands upon her shoulders and throat and breasts. There was no hurry; no surrender to urgency; no heedless demands—only the building symphony of caress and approach and readiness. Then, in the age-old ritual of culmination, he was with her.

She gasped in delight and rolled her head. She looked vaguely beyond the bed and into the closet. She saw a woman's dress hanging there by his robe. Had he lied about living alone? Who usually shared this bed with him? Where was she tonight? Did she know?

Cal's hand cupped Ann's chin and turned her face so that she looked up at him. His mouth closed over hers for a long, intense moment.

"Like this!" he said. "I'm your man and don't you ever forget it."

"No ... no ... no ..." Her voice was a moan, and she did not know if she spoke to refute his claim, or to confirm his command, or to cry against her own helpless, ecstatic surrender.

They were awakened before ten o'clock the next morning—unusually early for both of them. A bedside telephone rang for the third time before Marker answered it. He spoke softly for a moment and hung up.

"Sorry, baby," he said to Ann. "I have to meet Jerry. A friend of mine's in trouble with the law."

Ann stretched luxuriously. She glanced at the electric clock on a bed table and saw the time. Actually they had come to the apartment reasonably early, and had probably been asleep by two o'clock. Their love-making had been eager and quickly exhausting.

"Almost eight hours of sleep," she said as she stretched. "Cal, I feel *good*!" She wondered if the "friend" was one of girls. Maybe it was the girl who owned the dress in the closet. The thought gave her a strange, perverse pleasure.

He glanced at the clock, the quizzical smile and lifted eyebrow indicating his own, obvious thoughts.

"We'd better not," he decided. "We have to eat. I want to take you home—it's on the way—and I have to be on time with Jerry."

He pulled her to him and for a moment she thought he would abandon his good intentions, but he released her with a small laugh.

"Take your shower," he said. "I'll put coffee on and shave."

She showered quickly and dressed. She opened a medicine cabinet to look for a spare toothbrush and found one still in cellophane. There also was a woman's deodorant and a small package of bobby pins. The remainder of the contents of the cabinet were masculine. A twin cabinet over the built-in dressing counter caught her attention. Tentatively she opened it. The contents were entirely of a feminine nature.

Thoughtfully she closed the cabinet and left the bathroom. She was certain that Cal Marker had lied about a woman living with him, but she told herself that it didn't matter. She was not going to listen to his propositions.

She was thankful to him for what he had done the night before, and she had tried to repay him in the only way she could. But she would not accept his permanent protection; she would not live with him; she would not become his head chick; and— she told herself emphatically—she would not be in love with him!

She found him in the kitchen, shaving with an electric razor while he waited for coffee to percolate and toast to pop from a toaster.

"You can move in with me today," he said.

"Cal—listen to me. I'm sorry, but it isn't going to be that way."

"We won't argue about it now."

"Not now nor ever."

He smiled at her and finished shaving. She watched him for a moment, feeling a strange and disturbing affection for him, remembering how it was in bed with him, and almost wishing that he didn't have the appointment with the attorney.

"Pour the coffee?" he asked.

"Oh, yes." She found cups and poured coffee. There was butter for the toast in an icebox. They breakfasted quickly and with no more talk about his plans.

She insisted upon doing the dishes while he dressed. They rode to the basement in an elevator and he helped her into the Jag. Ten minutes later he parked in front of her apartment building.

"I won't come up," he told her. "But I'll call later."

Before she could answer, he had kissed her lightly and opened the car door for her. She got out and he said, "Later!" again and the Jag darted out into a hole in passing traffic.

She started to cross the sidewalk toward the building entrance and Casey Shean stepped from a parked car that she hadn't noticed and called to her.

She turned, saw him, and waited. He was smiling peculiarly and she was certain that he had witnessed Marker's kiss.

"I've been waiting for you," he said.

She smiled tentatively. What was there to say? That she had just come home from spending the night with a man who drove a Jaguar? That she had turned three tricks the night before, had been involved with a vice cop, had been forcefully propositioned by a pimp who wanted her to be his head chick and star?

"I've been out," she said lamely.

"I want to talk with you, Ann. I mean—maybe I *did* want to talk with you. It looks as if I might be a little late."

If she invited him up, the bedroom door probably was open and he would see that the bed had not been slept in. Maybe that was the thing to do—a simple way to tell him the truth. Only she knew that she did not want him to learn the truth about her.

"Casey, I'm sorry. I have a hair appointment," she lied.

"Well, then, just a few moments in my rented car?" he asked hesitantly.

She didn't want to talk with him now. She suspected what he might have to say, and in the last two days her life had become too involved for her to think clearly. On the other hand, she couldn't refuse him. He did mean something to her. Maybe he meant more than she realized. And she felt a necessity to explain away Cal Marker and the kiss.

"Just a few moments, then," she said. They went to the same car that he had rented for their trip into the country. He glanced at the parking meter that had flipped red on the indicator, and he put in a coin while she got in the car. He went around to the street side and got in and closed the door. He looked at her with the same uncertain smile he had worn since he first had greeted her.

"Maybe I'm just a small town boy," he said tentatively. "If I'm out of line, just tell me. If I'm intruding. Only after yesterday I thought—" He stopped speaking and his Irish smile lit his face, a little crookedly, as if he might be mocking himself.

"Ann," he said, very quietly. "I'll skip the build-up and talk straight. Is there any reason why you can't marry me and go back to Montana?"

Why did you have to ask me now? she thought. *Why now when my mouth still is bruised from Cal Marker's kisses, and my body still feels him, and my purse has a hundred and fifty dollars from customers I've been whoring with? Why now, Casey? Why didn't you ask it years ago and make me listen? I might have, Casey. I might have. But now I'd give you such a shopworn buy.*

"Casey, don't ask me that. Please. Not now," she said, almost frantically.

"There's someone else? The man who drives a Jag?"

"No. That's not what you think. He's—an old friend."

He nodded and his smile was gone. He lit a cigarette and the seriousness of his expression held a wisdom and sophistication that she had not quite expected.

"Think it over," he said. "If there's anything you want to tell me, you can. I wasn't born yesterday, Ann. I wouldn't expect a virgin. I just want the woman I love."

She got out of the car, hurriedly, and blindly because her eyes suddenly had filled with tears.

"I'll call you late this afternoon," he said.

She nodded, turning away so that he would not see the tears, and walked quickly to the apartment building entrance.

"The woman I love." Casey—don't you understand? The woman you love is a fifty-dollar whore. She's for sale.

CHAPTER EIGHT

Her apartment had the fresh, tidied, orderly look of a place just cleaned. She realized she had this feeling about it because of the undisturbed bed and the slight staleness of air.

She automatically checked with her answering service. The only number and message had been left earlier in the morning by Casey. She hung up and went into her bedroom.

For a moment she debated about another bath, but she had showered less than an hour before at Cal Marker's. She got out of her clothes and put on skin-tight Capri pants and a peasant blouse, slipping her feet into ballet-type slippers.

After a moment's hesitation she dialed Clara's number. The black-haired girl's sultry voice answered. "Ann? Are you all right?"

"Fine."

"Darling, I was worried about you. I saw what happened in The Beard. You didn't see us. We were at a table. Then Cal followed you out. Tell me. What happened?"

Briefly Ann told her about the events in the parking lot.

"Did you go home with Cal?" Clara asked, a slight trace of irritation sounding in her voice.

"For a while," Ann said guardedly. "Is everything all right with you and Mike?"

"I guess so," Clara said wearily. "He's out for a while. He had to see his connection and cop some horse. I'm waiting for a call from the service. I think I've got a convention job lined up. Mike's been involved, too, and wants me to stick by the phone. Can I come down for a few moments after I get the call?"

"Clara, not if—" Ann left the sentence unfinished. She was cetain that Clara understood.

"I can afford to wait, hon," Clara laughed softly. "No. I just want to visit. Besides, I've your extra key. When I left the other day I picked up the wrong one from your dresser. I'll bring it back to you. Mike was here and let me in. And we've extra ones."

"I'm going to fix some lunch later," Ann suggested. "Come down and eat with me."

"I'd love to."

They hung up and Ann selected a stack of records for the phonograph. She would welcome some time alone to think, but she was glad that Clara would be down later, especially if Clara would restrict the visit to talking.

For one thing, listening to Clara's problems with Mike would serve to strengthen her own defense against Cal Marker. It was much easier not to want a man like Cal Marker when she knew what another man in the same circumstances was doing to another woman.

She stretched out on a couch and listened to the music, letting her thoughts flow aimlessly through her mind: Crowley, the parking lot, Cal Marker, Casey Shean, Cal Marker ... Cal ...

Her door chime sounded. She must have dozed. Clara probably had come down. She got up and went to the door and opened it.

Mike Lane pushed the door open wide and walked in, closing the door carefully behind him.

"Hi, chickie!" he smiled. It was obvious that he had recently had a fix. It showed in his eyes, his false buoyancy, his extreme self-assurance.

"Clara's waiting for you," she said trying to block his way. "You'd better hurry."

He shook his head. "She can wait. Who needs her, anyhow?"

"You do, Mike," she said levelly. "You and the monkey on your back."

"Like knock it off, chickie?" he smiled. "We know what I'm talking about. You're like ready, chickie. We could make it. You and me."

"Why don't you cut out of here?" she said coldly.

He deliberately inspected her, his eyes lingering at the low and wide neckline of the peasant blouse, down the outer smoothness of her hips in the tight Capri pants, along the inner lines of her thighs.

"I go for you, chickie. Like way out. How's to make it with me now? Let me convince you."

"Get out of here, Mike. You know how it is with Clara and me. Now please get out."

"Yeah," he smiled. "Maybe I know how it is with you and Clara. Like maybe she's got a yen for you. You're not les, are you, chickie? Not *you?*"

"Get out!"

"I'm going nowhere, baby. Not for a while. First we're going to make it, you and me. I want to convince you what a sweet daddy I'll be to you."

She saw his intention to reach for her and she tried to avoid his hands, but she was too late. She was startled and frightened by the strength of his thin, drawn body.

There was no brutal struggling. With cruel, painful force he twisted her arms behind her and pulled the loose peasant blouse over her head and back.

She wore no brassiere and his coat jacket was rough on the tenderness of her exposed breasts. She tried to turn her head away, but he held her chin with one hand as the other twisted an arm until her lips opened in a cry that he smothered with his open mouth.

The hand dropped from her chin and found the zipper on the Capri pants and she felt the garment go loose around her waist.

She fell to the floor, managing to break loose from him for a moment. He laughed and bent over her, pinioning her flat on the floor, her face twisting from side to side as he tried to kiss her again.

His mouth caught her upper lip and bit and she froze as the pain stopped her frantic struggle to get away. From the corner of her eyes she saw the apartment door open and then she looked over Mike's shoulder into Clara's narrowed, angry eyes.

Clara held the spare key to the apartment tightly in one hand as if she were about to throw it at the couple. Instead she tossed it across the room and slammed the door shut behind her. She stood motionless, glaring down at the couple on the floor; a furiously angry woman in an expensive cashmere sweater and the burgundy-colored shorts that she liked to wear around the apartment when she was alone or with Mike.

Mike looked up at her and slowly got to his feet. His expression was half amused, half angry.

"Where the hell did you come from?" he demanded.

"Can't she wait to get you on her bed?" Clara spat.

Mike had risen and was calmly lighting a cigarette, a sardonic smile twisting his lips. Clara's full attention was centered on Ann who had struggled to her feet and was trying desperately to zipper and hook the Capri pants. She realized the full implication of the scene in Clara's eyes, and she knew that the other woman was seething with anger.

"You bitch!" Clara said, the words deep in her throat. "You lousy little bitch. Behind my back. And I thought *he* was the one making the play!"

"Clara! It isn't what you think. He came in here and—"

"Knock it off," Mike interrupted. "Both of you. There's room for everyone. Even in bed." He laughed.

Clara ignored him, pushing past him as her clawed fingers slashed out at Ann's face.

Somehow Ann dodged the clawing hands and she grasped at the taller, black-haired woman. Her fingers caught the cashmere sweater. Instinctively she pulled and twisted, trying to throw the larger woman off balance. The sweater tore down the front completely exposing the other woman to the waist.

Ann screamed sharply as Clara's slender fingers found a breast and squeezed mercilessly. She broke away with frantic strength and beat into Clara's rage-distorted face.

They fell to the floor. The torn sweater bound Clara's arms for a few seconds. She flailed her arms angrily, trying to get at Ann's face, muttering short, obscene, angry expletives.

Clara's fingers hooked into the waistband of Ann's Capri pants. The grasping fingers pulled down sharply and the silken material ripped. Ann tried to scratch at Clara's face.

Then, suddenly Clara was astride Ann, her fingernails poised above the blond woman's face, her eyes flashing in feminine rage.

"I'm going to fix that pretty two-timing face but good!" she gasped, breathless from the struggle "I'll fix it so Mike nor any John nor anyone will want to look at it."

Ann gathered her tired strength into a last convulsive effort to free herself. She swung one bare leg high, trying desperately to hook it under Clara's chin, to force her back.

Above them Mike laughed insanely, obviously enjoying the struggle, delighted with this turn of events.

Clara evaded the swinging leg, rising with Ann's convulsive movement, and slapping the smaller girl sharply across the face, forgetting to claw, only wanting to hurt.

"Bitch!" she cried. "Yarding behind my back. Georging my man. You bitch, bitch, *bitch*!"

She raised a clawed hand to scratch into the unblemished soft skin of Ann's face. Ann shreiked in sudden fear and desperately rolled her face from side to side.

Mike abruptly stopped laughing. He reached down and in a quick display of strength he caught one of Clara's arms and pulled her away from the exhausted girl on the floor.

"That's enough!" he said sharply. He whirled Clara around so that she faced him. "Now you can fan that ass of yours back upstairs. You've had it."

"Mike! You can't do this to me. Damn you, Mike! I'm your woman. You can't want her!"

He laughed and took off his coat jacket and gave it to her.

"Put this on so they won't kick us out for your running around the halls without any clothes. And get the hell up there."

"Mike—I won't. I swear to God if you do this to me, I'll—"

He slapped her, hard and mercilessly.

"Cut out," he snapped. "Now."

"Mike—please! Not to me. Don't do this to *me*!"

He pulled her to the door, threw the coat over her shoulders, and shoved her out into the hall and slammed the door after her.

Sobbing with exhaustion and the trauma of the moment, Ann had got to her knees and was trying to stand, clutching the torn Capri pants entwined around her lower legs.

Mike crossed to her silently and jerked her up to her feet. He smiled at her and then slapped her smartly. She recoiled and looked at him with dazed eyes.

"Now we'll make it together," he said. "Now's the time."

"No!" She tried to claw at his face as she twisted against his grasp. He slapped her again and released her with a vicious shove. She tripped over the Capris and fell again.

He reached down and grasped the soft cloth of the single garment and ripped it from her legs and over her feet.

Ann evaded his clutching hands and got up and ran toward the bathroom. If she could get in there she could lock the door. She had taken only a few steps before he caught her and twirled her around so that she faced him.

His mouth clamped on hers with bruising force. A hand sought a breast. She fought him desperately, sobbing with anger and fright.

She managed to get the palm of a hand under his chin. She pushed up, forcing his head back.

"Damned bitch!" he swore. His hand left her breast and twisted her prying arm so that it came up behind her in a painful arm lock. She gasped with pain and was held helpless against him.

"Damned bitch," he said again. "Now you're for it."

He turned her with force on the twisted arm and pushed her through the bedroom door to the bed. He shoved her hard so that she sprawled face down across the bed. She tried to roll away from him, but he caught her and pinioned her, face up, as he knelt over her.

"This is rape," she gasped.

"Not after it starts, baby," he grinned. "I'll make you like it."

He took her almost within the moment, relentlessly, brutally, angrily, and solely to appease his lust. Ann felt pain and brutality.

She shut her eyes and fought nausea. Never had she felt so used, so utterly degraded, so much an animal being used in service by a male.

Twice he slapped her when she failed to please him in her frigidity.

"Make it with me, damn you!" he breathed harshly.

In desperation and fright she tried to do what he demanded and the revulsion and sickness inside her increased. His hands were cruel. His mouth was undisciplined and dangerous. Ann rolled her head from side to side in anguish. Again he slapped her.

Then his excitement burst in a final moment of brutal frenzy, and as suddenly as he had taken her he was through with her.

After he had left, she lay on the bed, too exhausted to bring her aching thighs together, conscious of the pain in her face from the slaps, the struggle with Clara, the treatment she had received in this room from a heroin-and sex-incited pimp named Mike.

She remembered his words as he left her: "I'm your sweet daddy now, chickie. You like it with me. You made it good with me. And from now on you're my head chick, and Clara's one of the cows. She knows it already, chickie. She knows it. And I'll see you later tonight. Maybe I'll fix you up for some tricks."

He had spoken to her in a quiet, smug voice, looking at her body as he spoke, finishing a neat knot in his tie, completely indifferent to the revulsion and hate mirrored in her eyes as she had glared at him. He had closed the apartment door quietly after him, still wearing the smug smile, still indifferent to what she might have felt about him.

After a while she managed to get up from the rumpled bed and go to the bathroom. She was sick, vomiting until her throat ached. When the sickness had left a little she rinsed her mouth and turned on the shower. She needed the solace of a bath now more than ever. A cleansing, healing, washing-away bath.

When she came out of the bathroom in a terry robe, her telephone was ringing. She answered it and a man's voice said, "Ann?"

"Yes. Who is this?"

"Your friend, Jim. The regional manager is here on his annual inspection. You remember him, maybe."

"I remember him," Ann said, trying not to let her weariness creep into her voice. There still was rent to pay, doctors to pay, expenses, and a living. Money for living. "The ends" they called it in the rackets, and she had to have "the ends" even when she'd been beaten and raped. No one cared particularly why you couldn't pay when you owed the money. People just wanted the money.

"Around nine tonight?" the man asked.

"That'll be fine."

"He's at that new deluxe hotel on the edge of town this time. Will you have any trouble. Can you get out by taxi?"

"They're a little edgy about girls arriving in taxis," Ann told him. "I'll drive out in my own car. What unit number?"

He told her.

"I'll find it," she said. "I've forgotten his name."

"Morton."

"I'm certain Mr. Morton will have a good time."

"Is your address the same?"

"Yes."

"There'll be two twenties and a ten in the mail. Right?"

"Exactly, Jim. Thank you."

She had hardly put down the telephone when it rang again and she answered.

"Cal, baby," Marker said. "You all right?"

For a second she was tempted to tell him about Mike and Clara and what had happened, but she sensed that this could only lead to more trouble, revolving around her. She had experienced enough for one day. If Mike persisted in his attentions, she might appeal to Cal Marker, but this would only place her even more under his protection and set him up as her man.

As for Clara—time would have to take care of that. Clara's angry storm had resulted as much from her sense of inadequacy in losing Mike, or in just the fact that Mike would dare to make passes at Ann. To sustain her own pride, it was better to blame Ann. She could make herself believe it. She had found them in a compromising position on the floor, with Ann much less than half clothed, and Mike obviously not trying to break away.

These facts already had gone through her mind before Cal had called, so her answer was half determined even before he had asked it.

"Yes, I'm all right, Cal," she said.

"Good. Incidentally, there was some guy sitting in a parked car watching us when I let you out this morning. He wasn't a roller, was he?"

He had seen Casey, she thought. "I guess not," she said. "Nothing happened."

"I just wondered."

"Did your trouble get cleared up?"

"One of the reasons I called you. I'm in a jam."

"With the cops?"

"No, not me. It's one of the girls. She doesn't mean anything to me, I mean. All business. Not like you. But she got involved in a shooting last night and they're holding her for a while."

"Oh?" Ann wondered what this had to do with her.

"The point is she was lined up for a two-hundred-dollar trick tonight. She's going to miss out."

"That's tough. Two hundred isn't easy to pick up."

"That's why I called you. I want you to take it. You'd be getting me off a spot, and in this case, the two bills are yours."

She thought about it for a moment. She still owed Cal Marker some favors for the Crowley affair.

"What can I lose?" she agreed. "But I've a trick lined up at nine. I don't want to disappoint him."

"This other isn't until around eleven or later. A few big spenders at a convention."

"There won't be more than one?" she asked, suddenly suspicious.

There was a brief silence, and then his voice low and persuasive.

"It isn't exactly a trick—not in the usual sense. There's another girl and—"

"Not a circus, Cal. I won't do it."

"Just once, baby. That'll square things for keeps. I know how you hate that stuff. I understand. I know that you don't buy any part of that *les jazz*—and that's one reason I want you for my chick. You've got to understand that. But it's also why I know you could take on this act tonight simply as a business prop. Cold and for the dough."

"Cal—I said I wouldn't and I meant it."

"Okay, Ann. I went all out for you last night. I tangled with the fuzz because I go for you like that. But I'm not holding that up to you now. You more than repaid it afterwards. I go for you that way. So let's skip it. I thought maybe you wouldn't mind this once. It's a good customer and it usually means several grand a year from this guy. He stages conventions. Public relations man. But I'd rather skip it than get you down. And I don't want you to think that as my chick you'd have me hustling for you. I don't buy that, baby. Just a few big contacts that you can handle after I wire you in. I get around."

It was the second long speech she had heard him make, and when he finished the telephone seemed oddly quiet.

She pictured him at the other telephone. He would look like a young business executive talking with a client, not a pimp trying to get a girl to participate in a homosexual exhibition with another woman in front of a group of men.

She thought of her night with Clara. She thought of the way Cal's hand had clipped down on Crowley's shoulder, and she thought of the way Cal Marker had held her and kissed her and made love to her. After all, sex was a business when you made it a business, and what was the difference? A good craftsman should be able to do all things of the craft well.

"All right, Cal," she said.

"Ann, don't say it unless it is all right. I mean what I said. You're my girl. I mean it."

"It's a business, Cal. I'm not your girl," she said. "You helped me last night. I'll help you tonight. It won't mean anything—like you say."

"Afterwards we'll have the rest of the night, baby."

"Let's talk about that later. Where do I go for this?"

"They've got all of one floor at The Chateau. You'll perform in a three-room suite with the other girl—Yvonne's her name, and she's a star like you, just got her from San Francisco."

At the mention of the hotel name she felt quick apprehension. She did not want to run into Casey there, and it was very possible.

"Listen, Cal," she said hurriedly. "I'm nervous about The Chateau. The door knocker there had been watching me—"

"Rourke? That hotel click makes more out of a few of us than he does from the hotel. But if you're nervous go in the side door. Go straight up to twelve-o-one. Ask for a guy named Art Munson. He's the public relations guy running the show. He'll know who you are."

"At eleven?"

"Right. I'll be at The Beard when you've finished. Art will pay you before you leave. You can get the other details from Yvonne. She knows all the tricks. Just do what she suggests."

"All right, Cal. This once."

"That's my chickie," he said softly. "I'll see you later."

She heard the telephone click and thoughtfully she replaced the instrument in its cradle.

Just this once, she told herself. *And you're a fool to do it.*

Even as she chided herself, she knew that she would go through with it exactly as he wanted her to; just as he had planned it; so confident that he hadn't bothered to be anything but obvious in his asking.

Then—for no apparent reason—she felt a small chill so sharp that she actually shuddered.

CHAPTER NINE

The slamming of doors, tinkle of ice against glasses, sound of men laughing, talking, guffawing; the odor of cigarette and cigar smoke, of whiskey and gin; the blare of a television turned on and forgotten; the hurrying back and forth of bellboys with trays; the noises, odors, voices, and confusion of a convention after a day of meetings—all of these were familiar to Ann as a tall, balding young man with dark brown eyes and a perpetual smile on his lips introduced himself as Art Munson and took her in charge.

"Yvonne is waiting for you down in twelve-sixteen that's a suite we have set up. We moved all the furniture except for a mattress on the floor and chairs. We rigged up a lamp. Makes it like an in-the-round theater setup—if you know what I mean."

"I know what you mean," Ann said cryptically. Disgust already was making her regret her decision. Some girls liked exhibitions, or at least they didn't mind them, and they thought they always got more out of the men for the tricks afterwards.

To put herself on display was revolting. For anyone else but Cal—well, she had *promised* him. Even if she was a fool, she would. At least it wasn't an exhibition with a man. With two women it could be nothing but rehearsed phoniness.

Yvonne was a small, neatly molded girl with very black hair and eyes. She was possibly a couple of years younger than Ann, and she already had taken off her dress and was sitting in a straight chair glancing through a newspaper.

In the center of the room was a mattress covered by a white sheet. A reading lamp had been situated to throw its circle of light on the mattress.

The small, dark girl glanced up and smiled at Ann.

"Hi, Ann," she said. "Cal said we could work this out." She glanced at Art Munson with a meaningful look. "Why don't you leave us two girls alone for fifteen minutes or so before you bring in the panting mob. Okay?"

"Sure. And look, baby—before you're through tonight—"

"On the house?" Yvonne asked.

"I think I could find an extra fifty in the expense account," he winked. "And one for you, too, Ann, for a man I'll point out to you. He's the boss. He likes blondes. The rest of what you pick up—besides the two bills for the show—is what you can get from the boys. I've pegged it at fifty a trick. Okay?"

Yvonne nodded for both of them and Munson winked at them and went out taking a last look at Yvonne in black, lacy undergarments.

"Square," Yvonne said disdainfully after he had left. "If he'd wanted it on the house, it would have been the quickest trick I ever turned. Cal says you're new with the circus stuff. I'm a les. I don't mind. But don't worry. This is strictly for dough. I don't go for your type."

"You'll have to tell me what to do."

"Get out of your dress. We'll rehearse. I know what makes them pant."

Hesitantly Ann got out of her dress. Then, within a few moments, Yvonne demonstrated with such a skilled objectivity and professionalism that their rehearsal seemed as unexciting and routine as two girls going over a dance routine.

"Just make like it's crazy with you," Yvonne advised when they finished. "I don't think it's so much what we're actually doing—or appear to be doing—that gets 'em as much as how we appear to react. Christ! Men are creeps! Getting their kicks watching two women perform."

"All of them?" Ann asked curiously.

"Maybe not all, but a lot. Of course, they're hot for you afterwards. Maybe they think you're all warmed up for them. So it's part of the business and another way to make a buck. We better get these flimsies off. They'll be here any time."

The only light was the glow from the reading lamp on its standard. The overhead lights had been turned off. The room was hot from the pack of bodies in it. Cigarette smoke was heavy, looking blue under the light and over the two women on the mattress. There was a sound of quick, eager breathing of roused men, with an occasional hard cigarette cough, or the sound of ice against glass.

At first there had been talk. Crude wise-cracks. Uneasy talk as if the men were embarrassed to be there. Then the talk died down as the men riveted their attention upon the small circle of lighted area.

Ann felt completely detached from that circle of light. She felt almost as if she were watching, or as if she were taking part in a play without words. She moved almost mechanically. She did the things expected of her. She kept her eyes shut for the most part. She let Yvonne carry the brunt of the activity and took the part of passivity.

They were almost finished. She simulated the intense reaction Yvonne had suggested. Behind the background of heavy breathing she heard the door open and a man's voice.

"They've got a show going on in here. Let's take a look."

"Look, Bill—I've got to get to bed. I've business in the morning, and—"

"Business? Sure! At our salesroom! It's a break you're here during the convention—"

"For Christ's sake shut up!" someone whispered. "Either get in or get out. We've got something going here."

"Okay, okay. We're in. Hey, Casey—look what they've got for us here!"

On the mattress Ann became frozen into immobility. She felt Yvonne's hand suddenly press upon her in urgent warning, and automatically she responded with her simulated response.

She kept her eyes tightly shut and tried to turn her face away from the door she had heard open.

The man named Bill said, "What the hell, Casey. Let's watch it!"

The door slammed shut and Bill said, "Guess he's got a weak stomach."

"Shut up!" someone hissed. The breathing in the room became more uneven and strenuous and there were a few nervous laughs.

A tight, eager voice said: "Look at the blonde. It's really got her. She's crying. Look at the tears. She likes it, that baby does!"

Several men laughed uncomfortably and Yvonne pretended to go into a fenzy of motion. Somehow she managed to grasp the cord to the lamp and pull it. The room plunged into darkness, as Art Munson and Yvonne had planned it.

A moment later when Munson snapped on the overhead lights, the two girls were standing and putting on robes that Yvonne had brought. Munson stood protectively between them.

"That's it, boys," he grinned. "And the rooms are twelve-ten and twelve-eleven. You're all in the electrical business. Let's see if you can shock the girls! Just give them a few moments first." He started to herd the men out of the room. Yvonne went toward the bathroom with Ann.

"What went wrong, hon?" she asked in a low voice.

"Toward the end. Jeeze! You really froze. Did I hurt you?"

"No. It wasn't you."

Yvonne looked at her closely, and a small expression of resentment came into her face. "I don't know what's bugging you, dearie, but don't blame me. It's just a job."

Ann shook her head and tried to smile. "It hasn't anything to do with you, hon. Believe me. It was something else—personal. I can't talk about it."

The smaller girl was immediately mollified. "Gee, if there's anything I can do, Ann."

"No. It's all right."

The dark girl shrugged. "Okay. It's your problem. Shall we get on with our tricks?"

Ann bit her lip and stared at herself in the bathroom mirror as she applied new lipstick. Now Casey knew. He had seen her at her worst. Worse than she ever actually was because this had been something beyond the pale for her, done to satisfy her debt to a man. Debt? Or was it attraction?

Whatever it was, it was done. Casey had seen her. He knew. He would despise and loathe her now. He would sicken at the thought that he had asked her to marry him. And maybe that was the way it was meant to be. Outside were a dozen or so men waiting to be served after a perverted appetizer.

"Yes, let's get on with our tricks," she said. "We've got work to do."

Yvonne grinned at her in the mirror. "Honey, I hope you can take it. From what I saw of that bunch, this is going to be the nearest thing to a gang-shag we've had in a hell of a long time."

They left the suite and each chose one of the two rooms. Art Munson was waiting for them in the hallway and he followed Yvonne into the room she selected, saying over his shoulder that he had some financial business to attend to first with her. Yvonne winked at Ann as she went through the doorway.

A heavy-set, slightly gray-haired man who looked as if he once had been a lineman or a construction boss was waiting for Ann.

"I'm the boss," he grinned.

They went into the bedroom and he turned the key in the lock. He began to undress, looking at her with the grin in broad evidence again.

"Rather have a man, wouldn't you?" he asked.

"Yes," she assured him. This was the correct business answer. The customer is always right.

"Well, you're going to have one, blondie. A real one. Right now!"

At 1:25 A.M. Ann took a down elevator. Yvonne had an all-night date with a salesman.

The lobby was almost deserted and Ann crossed quickly, looking to neither side, hoping that no one would stop her. Outside she found an empty taxi at the door, before a sleepy doorman could summon it, and climbed in. She gave the address of The Beard.

She didn't notice a car pull out from the curb behind the taxi, then follow the taxi across town to the night club. She didn't notice it as she got out and paid the cab driver and went inside. She looked over the crowd. Cal was sitting alone at a small table in one corner. Mike was at the bar with his young blonde. Clara was not in evidence.

Wearily Ann crossed the club and sat at Cal's table.

"You made out?" he smiled.

She looked at him steadily, and after a moment she allowed him a very small and tired smile as she shook her head. "I made out." She opened her purse and took out a small fold of currency. She counted it carefully and shoved half of it across the table to him.

"What's that for?" he asked.

"Your commission."

"No. That wasn't the deal. You helped me out."

"It's a business deal, Cal. Take it, or say good night."

He looked at her with the lifted eyebrow and then he shrugged and picked up the money. He counted out half of it and shoved it back at her. "You gave me too much. This is closer to an agent's fee."

"If I were your head chick, you'd be taking it all and I'd be getting nothing but the ends."

"You've got it all wrong, chickie. Believe me." He reached across the table and then glanced up over her head and his expression lost its pleasant smile. "Okay, chump? What's on your mind?"

Ann turned and looked up into the hard, angry face of Casey Shean. He was staring into Cal Marker's face, and his fists were clenched.

"Casey!" Ann cried. "Casey—what?"

"Come on," Casey snapped angrily. "We're getting out of here. I want to talk with you."

Marker stood and stepped out from behind the table.

"I don't know who you are, buddy-boy," he said quietly, "But she's not going anywhere with you." He looked down at Ann and said: "Who is he?"

"Stop it, Cal," she said. "He's an old friend. This hasn't anything to do with you. Keep out of it."

"I don't like squares who push regulars around," Marker said.

"Then you won't like me," Casey smiled thinly. "Because if you get in our way I'm going to push your face in."

Cal had the same, tough, uncompromising look Ann had seen on him when he had manhandled Crowley. If Casey started a brawl in this place, anything could happen. Cal had dozens of friends in the place, and life was cheap to all of them.

Ann stood and smiled, hoping to dispel any curiosity about them from the regulars in the place.

"Cal, please take it easy. Casey is a very old friend. We went to school together and he's in town on business. He's going home Saturday."

She turned to Casey and said, "Cal hasn't anything to do with what's on your mind. Drop it. And forget me. I think we both know why. It's all over now."

"I'll decide that," Casey said. "Are you coming out with me, or do I pick you up and carry you?"

"Chump, you're asking for it," Cal said sharply.

"All right. We'll all go out," she said. "Let's not start anything in here. There's nothing to be started."

Somehow she managed to get them walking toward the door. They went outside and stood on the sidewalk a few yards from the entrance of the club. The street was deserted.

"No," Ann said coolly, "there's only one thing for you to say to me, Casey. That's 'good bye.' We both know why."

"We're going to talk about it. Alone," he said, looking at Cal Marker.

"All right, I've had it, chump," Marker said in a low voice. His hand came up to make the hard, chopping judo motion. Ann caught her breath. She didn't want this to happen to Casey.

"Cal!" she cried. "Don't!"

"Sorry, baby," he said, and she knew he was about to strike.

Then Casey Shean struck with a lightning blow that she didn't even see. She did see the way Cal Marker staggered back, the surprised look on his face, and the way he fell.

She saw Casey reach down and pull Marker up and slap him hard in a forehand-backhand rapidity that almost sickened her.

"Taking her money! Pimp! Louse! Son-of-a-bitch! Making her do what she did tonight!"

Marker brought up a knee in vicious attack. Casey turned barely enough to avoid devastating damage, and the movement took him off balance. Marker threw a hard, fast jab that caught the Irishman on the side of the jaw. Casey floundered backwards, but managed to grasp Marker's coat to pull the man down with him.

They rolled on the sidewalk in furious combat. For seconds Marker straddled his lean opponent.

"All right, square," he snapped. "Let's see if you can take it!" Marker's fist started a rapid series of hard blows to the face below him. Only one blow connected solidly. Somehow Casey got a hand on Marker's throat. He squeezed. Marker gagged and twisted away.

They were on their feet again. Marker desperately tried to use the judo blows that had been successful against Crowley, but Casey obviously knew how to avoid them and counter with his own attack.

Neither spoke. They gulped air in the savage efforts of the fight. Casey's longer arms and reach began to make a difference. He scored repeatedly to Marker's head.

In a last desperate effort to reach Casey Shean with a judo blow, Marker came in too close to the taller man. The Irishman blocked the side-hand blow with his left forearm and crossed to Cal Marker's head with a hard right. Marker fell back, shaking his head to clear it, gasping for air.

Casey swung again and Marker went down, tried to rise, and fell back. He looked up at Casey Shean with hatred in his eyes.

Casey turned away from him. He took Ann by the arm and headed her toward his rented car parked nearby at the curb. "We're going to talk," he snapped again.

Behind him Marker got slowly to his feet and wiped blood from his cut mouth. He looked after the couple with a baleful glare.

"Take her and talk to her, you bastard," he said. "But she's mine. And she knows it."

She was too tired to resist him as he put her in the car, or to try to argue with him. She sat quietly in the far corner of the seat from him, staring dully at the avenue he had chosen

Finally he stopped in a quiet residential district, away from houses, under large trees. He turned out the car lights and killed the engine.

"I don't know where to begin," he said.

"Don't try to begin," she said. It was over. She might as well end it once and for all. "There isn't a beginning because there's only an ending. Casey, I'm a call girl. I'm a prostitute. I'm a whore. You saw me working tonight. You've heard me tell you. And now you know. You're only wrong about one thing. I have no pimp. Cal is not my man. If you saw me give him money, it was strictly business."

"Okay. Let that stand as you want to let it stand. Let everything be as it is. Whatever you call yourself. Whatever you think you are. It isn't ended."

"Are you crazy? Casey—I love you for asking me to marry you when you didn't know. I respect you. I couldn't have said 'yes'. I know that now. Because I couldn't do that to you, and I don't think I could ever have told you what I am."

"That's what I want to talk about."

"Casey—don't try. Just shut up. Shut up and take me home."

"No. Godamnit, now listen to this! That kid I roomed with. That kid I grew up with whose mother was a madam. I knew her well when I was a kid—and when I was older. When I was old enough to use her girls sometimes and for her to talk with me."

"No, Casey. Nothing makes any difference."

"This does. I learned about call girls, prostitutes, and whores—if that's the way you want to word it."

"Sure—I'll bet. But nothing like you saw tonight. Or do they have circuses in a mining camp like Butte, too?"

"Shut up and listen. I understand this. It's damned near clinical. She used to describe it that way, only she didn't say 'clinical'. But she meant that. It doesn't mean anything to you. I know that."

"So it doesn't mean anything to us. So what?"

"Listen to me," he said in a low, angry voice, clipping his words off as if he were using a sharp razor to separate them in each sentence. "Anatomical sexual intercourse can be as impersonal and functional as any impersonal service rendered. And it can also be one of the most profound experiences a man and woman can have together. I think it is for us. I don't give a damn what you've been. If I did I wouldn't be here now. You've got to consider this, Ann. There's something there for you, too. There was by the river on the bank. There was in Missoula. It hasn't anything to do with what you've done."

"Most men would think so, Casey. You should."

"What men? I've had probably twenty to fifty women. Most men I know have had several. Some a hell of a lot more. Read Kinsey. Read any of the surveys. So you were paid. Paid for services rendered. You gave nothing but the services of some muscles, some physical skill and bodily accomodation.

"You probably never experienced any pleasure. It's just a mechanical thing—a bit of sordid play-acting. But I don't like your selling yourself. I didn't like what I saw tonight, though I know it's part of the business. And I won't forget that I've had a fairly large number of women. And some I bought. I'm little different from you."

She shook her head. "No, Casey. You're trying to rationalize. You don't really believe this. You're mixed up."

"Mixed up hell. I can show you case after case in the West where men married prostitutes and madams and lived happy married lives."

"Casey—please shut up. Take me home."

"To that damned pimp?"

She drew up and looked at him with a sudden flare of anger. "I told you that he isn't, Casey. And that breaks it! Take me home. Damn you—take me home! I'm tired and sick—sick to death of you, Cal, and men. All the Goddamned men in the world!"

He seized her suddenly and roughly and kissed her until she stopped struggling and then he thrust her back into the corner of the seat.

"I love you—and shut up. I'm going to take you home. I'll see you tomorrow. You can start packing."

"You go to hell, Casey Shean."

He started the car and turned in the center of the street. He drove too fast in his anger, and after a few moments he reached out a hand to her arm and clasped it.

For a few seconds she resisted, and then she sighed in her utter weariness and let him draw her to his side. She shut her eyes and tried not to think, vaguely thankful for his arm around her.

She awoke when he stopped in front of the apartment house.

"Don't come in," she said. 'I've got to go to bed. I'm so tired. I'm sick."

"I'll call you tomorrow," he said. "And start packing."

She shook her head wearily and turned and crossed the street. She went into the foyer of the building. The elderly man at the desk stopped adding a row of figures on an adding machine and looked at her. He hesitated a second and then called her.

"Miss Freeman."

She turned from her direct route to the elevator and went to the desk.

"Yes, Mr. Waters?"

"I'm afraid—unless you've already heard, that is—"

"Afraid? Of what? Heard what, Mr. Waters."

"Your friend. That nice dark-haired girl. Miss Lundy."

"Clara Lundy? What about her?" Ann stared at the old man, trying to read the words in his eyes before he could speak them.

"It was terrible, Miss Freeman. She jumped from the window of her apartment. I thought you might have seen the stain on the sidewalk. The coroner said it was the worst—Miss Freeman! Here—use my handkerchief—"

For the second time within twenty-four hours Ann was violently ill.

The door chime was sounding. Finally she awakened herself enough to identify the sound. She looked at her bedroom clock. It was almost eleven. She had been sick and exhausted and she had slept the instant she had fallen into bed.

The door chime persisted. She got up, put on a robe and slippers, and went to the door. Mike Lane stood there, pale and drawn and needing a shave.

"Ann, I got to talk with you."

"I don't want to see you, Mike. It's no use."

"It's about Clara. I didn't know until I came home an hour ago. I was out when it happened."

"With that blonde?" Ann asked bitterly.

"Let me in, Ann. Please."

He looked ill. She supposed that he actually was in a state of shock. She could understand how he felt. She had been violently ill the night before when she had been told; down there in the lobby, with the old desk man trying to help her with his big handkerchief and his nervous, trembling hands. She remembered exactly what she had thought:

Maybe if I had called her ... talked with het ... let her be with me again ... explained about Mike. Maybe I did it to her.

And even this morning, as she faced Mike, there was a heavy weight of guilt upon her. She remembered the last time the three of them had been together and the things that had happened.

"Please!" Mike said. "I'm bogue. Sick. I need a fix, and I can't stay up there. I just copped and I need a place."

"Why not?" she thought. End it now. Let him in and tell him and end it.

"All right," she said. "Come in."

He entered the apartment and walked past her to the bathroom. He shut the door after him and remained in the room several moments. He came out holding his suit jacket under an elbow pressed against his side as he rolled down the shirt-sleeve of the other arm.

"Thanks, Ann. I had the works with me. I'll be all right now."

"Sit down," she said.

He sat on the couch and tried to smile. She looked at him, wondering if he saw the disgust and hate in her eyes. This man had raped her. This man had been responsible for the suicide of a friend. Worse—he had made her, Ann Freeman, a party to the suicide. He had made her one of the reasons why Clara finally had succeeded in ending one of her fits of depression with death.

Or was there more to it? Maybe if she had not rejected Clara, even after the fight yesterday, she might have stopped it all. Clara had wanted her, needed her desperately and she had turned her down.

Mike said, "Christ! It was a shock, Ann—she must have flipped."

"She was crazy about you. Why couldn't you be satisfied?"

"She should have known, Ann. She was head chick with me. She should have known."

"What was that stuff you were handing me?"

"What's that got to do with it?"

"Mike, I hate your guts. You made me help her jump from that window. She thought I was making a play for you."

"Don't try to tag *me*, baby. She had a yen for *you*. She was les, even when she got her kicks with me. What did you do to her? After that night she stayed down here with you? She told me. She was sore because of that blond chick, and she told me that morning. I know about the les party you two had."

"It didn't mean anything."

The dope he obviously had injected when he went into the bathroom was beginning to take effect. He was losing his extreme nervousness. Self-confidence was building rapidly in him.

"Ann, it's like we share something now. We can make it from now on."

"Like what?" Ann asked, feeling sick again. "Like you're asking me to take her place with you? When you've only known an hour that she's dead. When you probably made her do it? *Really* did, I mean. I wouldn't have hurt her for anything. And now you want me to take her place?"

"She flipped. It wasn't us. She just flipped. She always was from Crazyville. Just a mixed up kid."

"You're sick."

"How about it, Ann? We can make it. You know how it is with me. Like crazy in bed. So good you couldn't move afterwards."

"Oh, God—you bastard. Mike. Get out of here!"

"Play it cool, baby. We'll make it real good together. Wait and see."

Ann went to the apartment door, opened it, and faced the man.

"Get out," she said. Her voice trembled. "Before I yell cop. Before I put the Feds on you. Anything to get you out of my life."

For seconds he looked as if he might slap her, but what he saw in her face evidently stopped him. He let his lips curl into a forced almost theatrical sneer. He went to the door, slipping into his coat.

"So who needs you?" he said. "Who needs a two-bit chippie?"

She slammed the door hard after him and then wiped tears of anger from her eyes.

You've got to get hold of yourself, she thought. *You've got to get back where you belong.*

For several moments she stared at the closed door and then she went to her telephone. She dialed the coroner's office and asked several pertinent questions. She hung up in anger and disgust and dialed her attorney.

"This is Ann Freeman," she said. "I want you to do some things for me and don't ask questions—if you can do these things."

"I'll try, Ann," a deep, gentle voice responded.

"A friend of mine—Clara Lundy—killed herself last night. She's at the city morgue. They say someone should claim her body if she's to have a decent funeral and all the rest. A certain guy told them he wouldn't do anything about it. I don't think she had any relatives."

"A friend could do that, Ann."

"I don't want to go down there. I couldn't. But I want you to see that the body is claimed. You've got my bank account—the

emergency money. Take out a thousand dollars for her funeral
and a grave and a marker in a nice cemetery. They said a thousand will do it. Have the funeral Monday. She has some friends
who may come."

"If that's what you want."

"That's what I want," Ann said. She answered a few questions
and hung up.

She wasn't certain if she'd go to the funeral. There would be a
few people there, but not Mike. He had refused to claim the body
or to acknowledge Clara in any way.

If she thought she could stand it, she would go. Maybe by
Monday she would be all right.

Right now she had to fight back to her normal pattern of living. A week ago things had been easy. Casey had not come back
into her life. She had not met Cal Marker. Mike hardly looked at
her a second time.

She had to get back to what it had been then. Somehow she
had to get right side up again, back in balance, business as usual.
Maybe she could think clearly again when she knew who she
was, what she was, and what she wanted to do.

She got out her black book. She'd begin by rounding up some
business at once. She began to call numbers. These were men she
could call with a friendly gesture of not having heard from them
for some time. "… wondering if you are all right." Invariably a
few would rise to the bait.

Within the hour she had a matinee for three o'clock and a
midnight date with a man whose wife was out of town.

She fixed some lunch and before she had finished eating it
the telephone rang.

"Ann Freeman?"

"Yes. Who is this?"

"Mac suggested that I call you."

"Mac?"

"McClintock."

"Oh, yes." She occasionally had calls from McClintock, a so-called public relations man, but he usually referred, or had referred, them to Clara. The point was that she knew him and she was satisfied that the man on the telephone was a prospective John and not some enterprising vice cop.

"My name is Martin," the man said. "I thought you might like to—er—talk over some business tonight?" He sounded nervous. Possibly this was out of his line, or else he was very eager.

For an instant she was tempted to turn him down, but she reminded herself that she was going back to work, to bring things back to normalcy. He was a John and she had bills to pay.

"I'd like to talk business," she said. They set a time and place and she hung up.

Before she could turn away, the telephone rang again.

"Are you packing?" Casey Shean asked crisply.

"No, Casey, I'm not. Please leave me alone." There was no point in telling him about Clara.

"I won't take that for an answer."

"When do you leave?"

"I'm supposed to leave tomorrow. I can get two reservations."

All right. Tomorrow. Just give me time to get back into my own little orbit again. Then I can say 'no' better. No to you, Casey, and to Cal Marker. Let me do my work this afternoon, and tonight; and tomorrow morning I'll be Ann Freeman again, call girl, unencumbered by man.

"Let me have until tomorrow, Casey. Leave me alone until then. Give me a chance. That's all I ask right now."

"Fair enough. Tomorrow morning," he said. "And remember, Ann—I love you and I want you."

Thoughtfully she left the telephone and went to the bathroom. She ran bath water into the tub. She had the matinee for this afternoon. She had the midnight date, and she had the date with Martin. Three. She wasn't certain how many paying tricks she'd had for the week. She had to be practical now and forget Cal Marker, and Casey, and Mike Lane.

Even a call girl should keep up her bookkeeping. Two on Monday—Blen—Calman's customer. Maybe nine so far. She wasn't sure. The convention night had been crazy, and she had been upset about Casey. She had some payments coming by mail, too. Clara used to mark them in a book—each trick, with initials, and a date. Well, call it nine.

She must not think about Clara. That was a thing of the past now. Maybe Monday she would go to the funeral—the funeral she had given her friend Clara. Maybe Clara understood all of it now, and accepted this last gesture of friendship.

In the warm drowsiness of the bath she shut her eyes:

When I was a little girl I thought all the people who had died were everywhere around us as spirits, watching everything we did. If that's so, my ancestors probably all are shocked—if they've been watching me. Or were there other whores in the family line? Or did they call them sporting girls back then? Or demimondes? How far back? How many centuries ago in family lines have there been mistresses and loose women and fallen women and seduced girls and unmarried pregnant women and unfaithful wives and chippies and whores?

She opened her eyes and stared unseeingly at the ceiling of the bathroom. Remembering had suddenly become a dull, emotional pain. She remembered the night she had heard her parents talking in the privacy of their bedroom—the intense childhood need for love and security that she never had found.

"So now I have this," she told herself angrily. "This! And I hate it. I'm unclean. All the baths I can take will never make me clean again. Not inside where it counts. And how can I get out now? How could I bear Casey—or any man—a child. A child to give the love I never had. What went wrong? Where? When?"

After several moments she wiped tears from her cheeks.

"Too late," she said aloud. "Too late."

She finished her bath and dressed, afterwards mixing herself a strong drink, which she seldom did. The liquor was warm and comforting.

Minnie arrived to clean the apartment, expressing embarrassed condolences about Clara.

Cal Marker called at two o'clock.

"Rough about Clara," he said. "Do you want to talk about it."

"Not now, Cal."

"I thought not. Don't take it too hard. She was psychopathic."

"You think she was?" she asked, almost disdainfully.

"I think she was," he said crisply, as if he had detected and resented the snideness in her voice. "I've had enough psychology and seen enough nutty human frailties in my life to know."

"I didn't know you'd been to college," she said, wondering if he had.

"Forget it. You're busy?"

"A matinee and two dates tonight. Real busy. I'm getting over Clara. Making myself work hard. Nice and brittle and even a little gay."

"Don't overdo it, baby. You sure you don't want to see me? Maybe I could help."

She laughed bitterly. "Cal—not you, too!"

"Me, too, what?"

"Man's cure-all for every woman when she's out-of-sorts, emotionally disturbed, upset, unhappy, or not herself is: quote— a good lay is what you need!—unquote."

He laughed. "All right, chickie. You win. Will you make the scene later? Or call me here at my place. QUeen seven four hundred if you finish early."

"I don't know, Cal. I don't think I want to see you again."

"We'll talk about it."

She thought about Casey Shean. Tomorrow, Casey. Tomorrow, Cal. Everything tomorrow. Tonight was her balance wheel back to independent, solo, unattached, man-free Ann Freeman, call girl.

"Tomorrow," she said.

"Why not tonight? We can—"

"Tomorrow, Cal. Goodnight." She gently put down the telephone and broke the connection. After a moment she picked it up again and told her answering service to hold her calls.

She found Minnie in the bathroom.

"Try to finish by three," Ann said.

"Yes'm. I almost finished now."

3:15 P.M.

"How is business, Bill?"

"Terrific. The compacts are picking it up for us. I've been high volume dealer in this area for two years. It was getting tough, but the compacts gave us a shot in the arm."

"They're cute."

"If you like a small car. By the way, how about that car I sold you? Time for a trade, Ann. I can make a real deal for you now. Wholesale for you. I mean it."

"I'm satisfied with the car—and you. Why don't you see me more often?"

"You wouldn't try to con me, baby? Another old pro like me?"

"You're not a con artist—you're a salesman. There's a difference. You give value for the money—even if you take some of it back in high finance rates!"

"You're smart. I like that about you. Along with some other things. Like this ... and this ..."

"Do I give value for your money, Bill?"

"Yes—and why don't you shut up? H-m-m-m? Just demonstrate the ride, baby ... *That's* right. *That's* value—*real* value, baby!"

4:10 P.M.

"Mr. McClintock, this is Ann Freeman. Do you remember me?"

"I certainly do, Ann. You are—were a friend of Clara's. I just read about that. Terrible thing. What was she, psycho?"

"I don't know, Mr. McClintock."

"Her friend—Mike? Must have hit him hard. Too bad. Was there something you wanted, Ann? I've another call coming in—"

"Just checking. You know how it is. A man called me. He calls himself Martin. He mentioned your name."

"Martin? Sure? Wonder how he called you. He usually went to Clara and he knows that guy Mike pretty well. I might have mentioned you to him, though. And he might have seen the paper about Clara and—well, when a man like Martin's got the yen he's got to do something about it. You know how it is. But he's no cop. That's for certain."

"You sound as if—"

"Ann, baby a client just walked in. I'll call you one of these days."

The telephone clicked in Ann's ear. She hung up with a frown.

"Forget it," she told herself after a few seconds. "Mac's okay. He wouldn't set you up for a bust. If he okays Martin, you can take the chance. A John's a John and fifty bucks is fifty bucks and you spent twenty fifty-dollar tricks this morning. You need work."

She felt a slight glow still lingering from the drink she had mixed earlier. In the kitchen she found a bottle of vodka. If she needed drinks to help her through the rest of the night, she had better drink vodka. They said there was no odor from vodka, and Johns could be particular about drinks on a girl's breath—unless they had been drinking themselves.

She mixed three strong gimlets, feeling them almost as soon as she had finished drinking them.

There was time for a light dinner, and maybe another gimlet or two, if she still felt the need. Then she would see Mr. Martin. And after that she would keep her midnight date with the man whose wife was out of town. Possibly—if she called her answering service—there might be even more calls for her to make.

8:30P.M.

Ann got out of a taxi and crossed the sidewalk to the hotel entrance for her date with Martin. The drinks had helped, and still were with her, but she was nervous. Something was wrong.

"You're imagining things," she told herself, "Put on a smile and go to work!"

This was the smile that Ann Freeman wore as she walked toward the bank of elevators in the downtown hotel. Within hours a man would bring her down in one of those elevators, supporting her bruised body with a hard hand; the sadist who would say: "We'll take a walk, baby. Those drinks were too stiff.

All you need is fresh air." Obviously words intended for the operator's ears. And the man would take her out and put her in a taxi and send her home where she would crumple face down on the cold tile of the bathroom floor.

This was the Friday night that may have started the preceding Monday—or possibly one night years before when a small, heartsick girl who was supposed to be asleep in her dark bedroom heard her mother say: "*I never wanted children. You knew that. You deliberately gave me Ann!*"

And a father who replied in the darkness of the house: "*I didn't want her. I knew how you felt about children.*"

Friday night.

EPILOGUE — FRIDAY NIGHT

She opened her eyes. The bathroom tile was warm now from her blood. She was choking a little. She coughed and pain seared through her abdomen. When she moved she felt the raw smarting of a whiplash pattern across her skin. Painfully she looked at her watch. Ten-thirty-five.

He must have hit me low, she thought. *I ache. I hurt. What did he do to me?*

McClintock wondered why Martin called me. Martin usually called Clara. He knew Mike. Martin knew Mike. Mike knew Martin. That was it. Mike had called Martin. Mike had set her up. Not for a bust. For a queer, a sadist, maybe a killer. I need help.

Slowly, carefully, she got to her hands and knees, staring down at the pool of blood on the tile.

"Casey—" she said.

If she crawled back into the hallway to the living room and across the carpeted floor there would be a telephone. Dial zero. Ask for the hotel number. *Now I've got to rest. Why do I ache inside, so low, so much? Why am I so weak? What did he do to me?* She gently let herself down on the hallway floor. She had crawled that far.

In Missoula we played run-sheep-run. Ibbity, bibbity, sibbity-sab. Count out to see who's "it" for kick-the-can on a summer night. The summer you were twelve. Johnny Nelson from next door hiding beside you in the summer darkness under the lilac tree. Johnny putting his hands under your dress and reminding you of the way you had played doctor with him in the attic the summer before.

She ran her tongue around the inside of her mouth, She found a sore, torn spot on the underside of her upper lip. This must be the source of the blood.

Fifty dollars a night. Fifty dollars a trick! Fifty dollars to lay a broad and beat her till she's sick. Almost two hours of it. She laughed a small hysterical laugh at the inane verse that seemed to pound through her mind with the heavy pulsebeat of her heart.

"Oh ... oh ... I can't—" she moaned. "Casey—"

She got to her hands and knees and crawled again. She went through the doorway into the living room. The telephone was across the room. She stopped and swallowed hard, tasting the saltiness of her blood from the broken lip.

When did it really begin? Back in an attic with the little boy next door when you took off your dress and panties and he played doctor?

In Missoula on a spring night with Casey? Irish Casey? Did it begin then? Does it matter when it began?

She swallowed in desperate small gulps, fighting nausea. Across the room the telephone was a silent, loyal friend waiting to be picked up. She ached. She was sick.

You did this, Mike. Now I know you did this. You told this guy that I'd be good for what he wanted to do. Maybe you gave him the fifty dollars to do it good. That's the way your junkie mind would work when you've been crossed. Your obscene, rotten, killer mind. You killed Clara. Really. But now I'm getting out. I've had it.

For several moments she rested on her back, staring at the ceiling, pressing her hands against her abdomen.

She rolled over and pulled herself up to her hands and knees again. Slowly she worked her way across the floor, and at last the telephone was within her grasp. She removed it from its cradle and stared at it.

Casey's rugged Irish face was vivid in her mind. She remembered his words. She remembered her promise of "tomorrow."

Tomorrow is Saturday and Casey wants to leave. But Monday is Clara's funeral. Someone said it, some place, sometime: "You can't go back."

Slowly Ann smiled and blood trickled gently from her torn lip, over her swollen lower lip, and down her chin.

"Face up to what you are," she said softly to herself.

She reached for the telephone and put it on the floor so that she could see to dial. Firmly she held her lips together as she selected numbers with a trembling finger. She finished dialing and she heard the ringing signal. After five rings—she counted them—a man's voice said, "Hello."

Once more she swallowed hard, so that she could talk, and wiped blood from her lips with a lick of her tongue.

"Cal," she said. "Cal—I'm hurt. Come and get me—"

www.ingramcontent.com/pod-product-compliance
Lightning Source LLC
Chambersburg PA
CBHW030126260626
47156CB00008B/2808